SHIFTR: SWIPE LEFT FOR LOVE (BOOK 1: DINA)

SHIFTER DATING APP ROMANCES BOOK 1

ARIANA HAWKES

Copyright © 2015, Ariana Hawkes

ISBN: 9798683595524

Imprint: Independently published

Cover Art by Covers That Pop

www.arianahawkes.com

All rights reserved

No part of this publication may be reproduced, distributed, or transmitted in any form or by any means, including photocopying, recording, or other electronic or mechanical methods, without the prior written permission of the publisher, except in the case of brief quotations embodied in critical reviews and certain other noncommercial uses permitted by copyright law.

This is a work of fiction. Names, characters, businesses, places, events and incidents are either the products of the author's imagination or used in a fictitious manner. Any resemblance to actual persons, living or dead, or actual events and businesses is purely coincidental.

SHIFTR: SWIPE LEFT FOR LOVE (DINA)

SHIFTER DATING APP ROMANCES BOOK 1

CHAPTER 1

"Lauren, I barely even know how to use email," Dina said. "I don't think this 'app' dating, or whatever you call it, is going to work for me." She flung her phone down on the sofa, and gazed around her cozy, tastefully-decorated apartment. She'd long ago resigned herself to being single, and she'd worked hard at making her surroundings as comfortable as possible. She wasn't even sure that she wanted to disturb the calm that she'd created for herself.

"Dina, when's the last time you had a date?" Lauren asked. Her voice was calm, but her eyes were sparkling with amusement.

"Um, there was that time when I went out for dinner with the guy who works at the DHL office," Dina said.

"And how long ago was that?" Dina counted on her fingers.

"Maybe a year ago?"

"Exactly!" Lauren said, in a tone of satisfaction. "Dina, you can't sit here alone, night after night, wasting your life, when there are so many great guys out there you could be having fun with."

"I don't know. I just feel so inexperienced at the dating game. I thought things were going to be forever between Trey and me. And we met at high school, so we didn't ever had to deal with any of that artificial, awkward dating stuff."

"And how many guys did you date before the DHL guy?" Dina joined her thumb and index finger together into an O shape. Lauren stared at her, her huge brown eyes open wide.

"You're saying you've never been on any other dates?" Dina shook her head sheepishly.

"Girl, we have to fix that right now! And you can stop looking like I'm trying to force you to go to the dentist, or something. Dating guys is *so* much fun," Lauren said. Dina took a gulp from her glass of white wine.

"I'm too old for this. Internet dating is something kids do. You know, people who actually look good in photos." Lauren's eyebrows shot up, halfway to her hairline.

"You have some crazy-ass ideas about things! You're a stunning, curvy woman. Look at you! And you're 36; you're in the prime of life."

"Yeah, that's why Trey left me for somebody almost two decades younger than me," Dina said, her voice sharp with bitterness.

"He left you for an intern in his office, right?" Dina nodded. "Trey left you because he's a weak man, and he couldn't handle a strong sexy woman like you. That's why he was chasing after teenagers. Now, let's forget about this asshole. He is over with. Will you at least try online dating? I promise you that there are lots of guys out there who will be so excited to meet you!" Dina glanced down at her phone.

"I don't know. I –" Lauren took Dina's hand, her eyes soft with compassion.

"Dina, I'm your best friend, and I love you. I wouldn't be suggesting this if I didn't think it was a good idea."

"I know," Dina said, and let out a long breath. Her hand crept over to her phone and she picked it up again. "Ok, I'll try it, but just for you. Tell me what I need to do?"

"Great!" Lauren came to life. She was at her best when she was helping people out. She took the phone from Dina and began installing several different apps. When she was done, she showed Dina her handiwork.

"Ok, an app on a phone is just like a button that helps you access a website real fast. So, I've installed Matchmakr for you," she said, pointing with an immaculately-manicured fingernail to a pink icon with a heart on it. "It's a good app, and lots of people like it. And there's definitely a lot of guys on there. And this one – " She pointed at a blue icon with a white wedding cake on it. "It's called *Find the One*. It's a great one for people who know they're ready to settle down, and are not just casual dating. I haven't used it myself, but it does have a good reputation. We can look at both of these, but there's one I just wanted to show you first." She pointed at an orange icon featuring what looked like an animal paw print, but the pad of the paw was in the shape of a heart. It was called Shiftr. She glanced sideways at Dina, and Dina noticed that her friend seemed unusually tense. Lauren placed her hand on her chest. "Dina, I know in my heart that this is the perfect app for you. But I need to ask you one thing: please be open-minded about what I'm going to show you. Can you promise me that?" Dina stared at her in confusion.

"Sure?" she said, shrugging her shoulders. Lauren pressed a purple-tipped finger on the little icon and the app opened. Dina shuffled closer, her curiosity piqued.

"In a moment, it's going to ask you to sign up, but first it'll let you take a sneak peek at a few of the guys." Lauren selected a couple of options, and suddenly the screen of Dina's phone was filled with the naked upper body of one of the best looking men she had ever seen.

"Wow!" Dina breathed. The guy's torso looked like it had been sculpted from marble, every muscle honed to perfection. He had shaggy brown hair, a strong jawline, and sexy eyes in an unusual amber shade. Lauren broke into a grin.

"See what I mean already, huh?" Dina nodded, too stunned to speak. Lauren flicked her thumb upwards, and a second guy filled the screen. He was also bare-chested, and his torso was the equal of the first one. He had dark brown hair, and mischievous-looking pale green eyes. Lauren flicked her thumb up again, and a guy with short black hair appeared. He had a lovely, handsome face, with delicious, chocolate-brown eyes, short black hair and a hint of a goatee. He had a sturdier body than their previous two, and his muscles looked powerful and meaty, like he did heavy, manual work for a living. "Girl, you're practically salivating," Lauren said, with a wicked cackle.

"It's just that I've never seen guys this hot in real life before," Dina said weakly. "But why are you showing them to me? They're way out of my league." Lauren shook her head.

"You are *so* deluded. Ok, I'm going to show you something

else now," she said, and swiped her thumb left on the phone's screen.

"What?" Dina said, frowning in confusion at the large black bear now filling the screen. Ignoring her, Lauren swiped back up to the brown-haired guy. She flicked her thumb to the left and there was now a big cat in his place. It was black, and green-eyed, and it looked coolly at the camera from its position up high in a tree. *Was it a jaguar?* Dina wondered dazedly, before Lauren swiped up to the first guy. Again, her thumb moved left, and the shaggy-haired guy was replaced by a large gray wolf, with amber eyes.

"What, so all these guys are nature lovers, or something?" Dina said. Lauren pressed her lips together.

"In a manner of speaking," she replied. "Did you notice that all of the guys look a little like the corresponding animals on their profiles?"

"Yeah! I guess they do, actually. So the photos are included in their profile to demonstrate their wild side?" Dina said.

"Pretty much. But it's more than that." Lauren swallowed. "Dina, what I'm about to tell you is going to sound real crazy, but please bear with me, and don't freak out."

"Ok?"

"These guys are all shape shifters. This means that they are half human and half animal, and they can shift between their human and animal sides at will." Dina's mouth fell open.

"This is a joke, right?" she said. Lauren shook her head.

"No, it's for real. It's a real site, and these guys are genuine shape shifters." Dina struggled for words.

"This is total nonsense!" she managed at last. "Lauren,

you're the smartest person I've ever met. How can you take this crap seriously?"

"I know this site is genuine, because it's how I met Connor," Lauren said. "Ok, look." She rummaged in her purse and pulled out her own phone. Dina watched as she tapped an identical paw print icon on the screen and the app opened. The first thing they saw was a photo of Lauren's handsome boyfriend. He was posed in a forest, leaning on a tree trunk, and he was also bare chested. Lauren swiped her thumb to the left, and in his place was a dark brown bear. Dina gaped.

"You're telling me that Connor is half man, half bear?"

"Yep!" Lauren said, her voice full of pride.

"I'm sorry, Lauren, but this is obviously a made-up story. You don't think he might be a bit of a fantasist?"

"I know it's true, because I've seen him in his bear form," Lauren said calmly.

"But, what? How?" Dina stammered.

"I knew he was a bear shifter, of course, since we met through the site. And, after a couple of dates, I was dying to see the other side to him. I realized that if I only ever saw him as a man, I was only getting half of him. One day, we went on a picnic in the forest, and he shifted for me. He stripped off his clothes, and one minute there was this hot naked man standing in front of me, and the next minute, there was a huge bear in his place. It was really cool."

Dina took Lauren's phone from her and swiped back to Connor, and then to the bear again, and back to Connor. As with the other guys she'd seen, the bear really did look quite a lot like Connor.

"This is the craziest thing ever," she said. "But why haven't

I already heard that there are all these guys everywhere that are half animal?"

"Because there really aren't that many, and it's a closely guarded secret," Lauren said. "When you sign up to the site, you have to sign a declaration that you won't tell anyone about shape shifters until you've found your match. And then, you're allowed to tell one person only, once they've been pre-approved by the site owners."

"You had me pre-approved?"

"Yes!" Lauren replied, the edges of her lips curving with mischief. "You're my best friend, and I knew this would be perfect for you, so you were my first choice."

"But, how did you get me approved?"

"I vouched for your character, of course, saying what a sassy, cool, warm-hearted woman you are. And I sent them a photo." Dina's heart jumped into her throat. She had a deep aversion to having her photo taken, to the point that she'd never even look at photos of herself.

"Which photo?" she asked, her voice taut.

"This one!" Lauren located it on her phone, and Dina forced herself to look. From the long red dress she was wearing, she deduced that it was from the last Hope Valley winter ball. But she had no recollection that the picture had been taken. As usual, she zeroed in on the things she hated about her appearance, like the fact that she was six inches taller than most of the other women there, and her huge boobs and wide hips. But, she had to admit, her hair looked pretty good; her black curls were tumbling around her shoulders, and she was smiling. Her smile was the thing she liked best about her looks.

"This photo got me approved to the site?" she asked incredulously.

"Yes! You look stunning," Lauren said loudly. "Don't even think about criticizing your appearance!" Lauren pressed another button on her phone. "Look!" she thrust an email message in front of Dina's face. It said:

Hi honeybun!

Thank you so much for sending this beautiful girl to us! She's so gorgeous and curvy. We'd absolutely love to have her on the site. I can tell the shifters will all be fighting for her the second she sets her profile up, so warn her to be well prepared!

How are things going with Connor? I just knew he'd be the perfect match for you!

Excited to hear from you!

Love and licks,

Tamika xoxox

"Wow!" Dina said, short of anything else to say.

"Shifters love curvy women like us," Lauren said. "Connor says it's the most perfect match imaginable – a rough, rugged shifter, and a strong, voluptuous woman. Kind of makes sense doesn't it?" she bumped shoulders with Dina. "And I can tell you, hun, my curves have *never* been worshipped like this before, in all my life!"

Dina's head was swimming with all the things she'd just heard. Sense told her the whole thing was crazy. But Lauren was not the kind of person who'd make things up. Was it possible that maybe, just maybe, there were guys out there who would appreciate her body? Who would not see her as second best? A tiny bubble of excitement bounced around inside her at the thought. She picked her phone up and looked at the first guy again. His sexy brown eyes seemed to be imploring her to get in contact with him. She swiped left to see his animal form again, and a message popped up on the screen: *Please register to continue locating your perfect match!*

"You've got to sign up now to be able to access the profiles," Lauren said, looking over her shoulder. "Let me help you." She took the phone out of Dina's hand. "I want to make sure you describe yourself at your best. Let me see – " She began typing. "Female. Height – 5'10?" Dina nodded. "Hair – black. Eyes – hazel." Lauren peered into Dina's eyes. "Or green, depending on the light. Hobbies?" She looked at Dina expectantly.

"Tutoring vulnerable kids," Dina said. "Interior design, dancing, hiking."

"Good," Lauren muttered as she typed. "And eating out."

"No, don't put that," Dina said.

"Dina, you love eating out. Your passion for food is a really good quality; don't be embarrassed about it. These guys aren't looking for some yoga freak, who exists on a diet of lettuce. They're looking for *real women*, with *real curves*, and *real appetites*, like us. Connor says my appetite is one of the sexiest things about me!"

"Ok, I'll take your word for it," Dina said, with a sigh.

"Now, tell me what you're looking for in a guy." Dina leaned back on the sofa and stared up at the ceiling.

"I don't know. Someone kind, caring, smart, who appreciates an independent woman. Someone who's passionate about what they do, no matter what it is. It'd be quite cool to be with a guy who works with his hands, but it'd be ok if he worked in an office, I guess." Lauren chuckled.

"Shifters aren't known for spending their lives cooped up in offices. There might be a couple of species that are ok with it, I guess, but most of them have physical jobs, like being craftsmen, lumberjacks, engineers, firefighters etc." Dina's eyes went dreamy.

"I've always fantasized about being with a guy who's a firefighter," she said. "They're so brave."

"Well, if you like, once we're done with your profile, we can search by firefighters," Lauren said, with a laugh. "What else?"

"A guy who wants a family, eventually," Dina said.

"Oh, that's a given. These shifters are all looking for their lifelong mate."

"Mate? What?" Dina yelped. Lauren fixed her deep brown eyes on Dina.

"If you get together with a shifter, you're not just boyfriend and girlfriend, or husband and wife, you're mates, and that's something really special. It's a very strong, unbreakable bond, which will unite the two of you on a deeper level than is possible between two mere humans. It guarantees you everlasting love and protection," she said. Dina shivered.

"It sounds like the daydreams I used to have when I was a little girl," she said.

"Exactly! Who didn't have those daydreams?" Lauren replied. "It was just a bit of a let-down when we all grew up and discovered that guys were more into lying around watching the game and drinking beer than getting the most out of a relationship. But Connor's not like that. He's so caring and attentive, and loves doing things in a couple. Family means everything to him."

Lauren had finished typing her latest entry. "Ok. Is there anything else you want to add about what you're looking for in a guy?"

"I don't think so," Dina said.

"Is there any species you're not willing to consider?"

"Umm, I don't know?" Lauren laughed.

"Of course you don't. This is all new to you. It's ok, we can add this bit later if you like. Now, you're supposed to describe yourself in five words, but I'm going to do this bit for you." Dina tried to grab her phone, but Lauren held it well away from her.

"Smart, funny, caring, sassy and warm-hearted. Right, that'll do." She stood up. "I'm going to use the photo of you in the red dress, but I'm going to take a couple of face shots too. Look at me." Before Dina could think twice, she was gazing up at her friend, and Lauren snapped several shots. "Perfect!" she said triumphantly. She sat down again, and Dina watched as she hit 'upload' and 'create profile'. An egg timer showed on the screen for a few seconds, and then, bam! There it was – Dina's complete, brand new profile. The full body shot was the main photo, and all her details were underneath.

"Where are the other photos?" she asked. Lauren swiped left, and a close-up of Dina's face appeared. Dina peered at it anxiously. The light from the window was shining right in her eyes, so they looked really green, you could see the scattering of freckles across her nose, and her lips looked nice and full. The way she was looking right up at the camera made her seem a little mysterious, as if she had a secret she was bursting to tell. She actually looked pretty cute, she admitted to herself.

"Sexy chica!" Lauren said.

"Not too bad," Dina said, blushing. Just then, a fluorescent pink heart popped onto the screen. Lauren gave a little scream.

"Oh my god, you've got an alert already! That has to be a record, girl!"

"What do I do?" Dina said, adrenaline fizzing in her stomach.

"Tap it, of course!" Dina tapped the heart with her finger, and the graphic burst like a balloon, leaving a message in its place: *Want to find out if we're a match?* it said, and it was followed by a happy face and a sad face icon.

"Ooh, he looks interesting," Lauren said, frowning at the thumbnail of the guy who'd sent it. "Click on his photo." Dina tapped again, and a photo of a stocky, muscular guy filled the screen. He had messy, dark brown hair, with the slightest hint of red, and a wide, angular face.

"He's really hot, but there's something a little arrogant about his smile," Dina said.

"I agree," Lauren replied. "It says he plays ice hockey, but when he's not doing that, he loves lounging around, watching movies. Mmm, I don't think that's the kind of guy I'd get on with. Let's see what kind of shifter he is." Dina flicked her thumb and a lion appeared, sauntering along a forest trail. "I knew it!" Lauren said. "I've heard on the grapevine that lion-shifters don't have an easy time finding human mates because of their very 'particular' personalities."

"Yeah," Dina said, biting her lip. "I can't believe I'm saying this, because he's insanely attractive, but I don't feel like he's the one for me. But how should I tell him?"

"Just tap the sad face icon, and he'll understand."

"That seems a little harsh."

"No," Lauren said firmly. "Shifters are very straightforward. One thing they don't do is play games. They understand that finding someone you're perfectly suited to is super important."

"Ok," Dina said slowly, and tapped the icon. Immediately, the lion's profile disappeared.

"You won't see him again now," Lauren said. "That's what's so great about this site. You don't have to scroll past the same old faces again and again. If you say *no thanks* to someone, they disappear, and if you see a profile you don't like when you're searching, you just swipe right, and they also disappear."

"That's so neat!" Dina said.

"Ok, this is the fun part. Tap 'search' and you'll start to see the profiles. You can order them by certain criteria, or you can just go random."

"I'll do that," Dina said, tapping 'random search'. A photo of a lean, black-haired guy filled the screen. He had powerful shoulders, and a muscular torso with narrow hips, forming a classic triangle shape. His worn blue jeans sat low on his hips, revealing those diagonal grooves of muscle that drove Dina crazy with lust.

"Wooh, he's hot!" Dina said. He had a nice face, with a strong jaw and firm lips, but there was something reticent in his eyes.

"What kind of shifter do you think he is?" Lauren said.

"Mmm, something canine, definitely. A coyote? Or a wolf?"

"My guess is wolf," Lauren said. Dina swiped left, and a wolf appeared, pale gray in color, with blue-green eyes. "Wolves are an interesting one. Because they live in packs, they have this really strict hierarchy. My guess, from the look of him, is that he's an omega, so will be of low status in his pack."

"Is that a bad thing?"

"No, not at all. It might mean that he's a very soft and devoted mate. It just depends on what you're into. Do you feel a connection when you look at him?" Dina shook her head.

"No. It's weird, but it's like I've got a voice in my head saying no."

"That was my experience when I was on the app too. With shifters, it seems that you just *know* whether they're suited to you."

"So, I'm going to swipe right, so I don't see his profile again?" Dina said. Lauren nodded, Dina's thumb flicked right, and he was gone.

The next guy had a shock of light blond hair that flowed down to his pecs, an unusual, angular face, and a sensitive, slightly wild look in his eyes. His muscles were long and lean, and his olive skin glistened, as if he'd just gotten home from a run.

"Is he a horse?" Dina murmured.

"Let's find out!" He was indeed a horse – a large, pale golden animal, with a broad white stripe running down the center of his face. His mane was exactly the same color as his hair. "He looks interesting," Lauren said.

"He looks like he'd be a lot of work to tame," Dina said with a giggle. "Maybe I'll leave him for later." She swiped down to the next guy.

Every few seconds, a message alert popped up.

"Wow! All these guys want to speak to me?" Dina exclaimed.

"Of course they do!" Lauren said. "But how about we have a little fun seeing what's out there first, before we find out who's fighting for your attention?" She temporarily disabled the alerts and refilled their wine glasses, and they hunched over Dina's phone, going from one guy to the next, to the next. The guys all had amazing bodies, with great muscle tone, and striking good looks, but beyond that, they couldn't have been more different.

It quickly turned into a game of 'guess the animal'. Most of the guys turned out to be wolf, bear, big cat, or stallion shifters, but there were also beavers, foxes, deer, and even seals and dolphins.

"This is so much fun," Dina said. "I feel like a kid in a candy store!" Lauren looked at her friend with affection, thrilled that she was enjoying herself so much. She'd known she wouldn't regret making Dina the one she shared the shifter secret with.

"What's the deal with shifters that live in the water?" Dina said, shuddering as she flipped between a photo of a surfer with long, tangled blond hair, and a shark. "How does that work?" Lauren laughed.

"I guess you'll have to move to whichever beach town they

live in, so they always have easy access to water!" she said. Dina kept staring at the shark photo. "I just can't see myself with a shark-guy," she said.

"Don't worry about it!" Lauren replied. "There are *plenty* of other options out there. What kind of shifters *are* you drawn to?" Dina flicked through a few more profiles while she was thinking.

"Well, the big cats are hot, but I get the feeling that they're too independent. I've always been more of a dog person," she broke off with a giggle. "Sorry, that was a terrible thing to say. The wolves are sexy, and I like the whole idea of being protected, but that hierarchy thing is probably a bit too much for me. But the bears – there's something lovable about them." She scrolled up to the last bear shifter she'd been. "They all seem to have these big, sturdy bodies, with meat on their bones. That's what I really love in a man, to be honest."

"Me too!" Lauren said. "When I first saw Connor, it was a no-brainer. I visualized those strong arms wrapping around me, pulling me against his hairy chest, and I just melted! Bear shifters are known for being reliable, protective and warm-hearted. They love the outdoors, and going hiking on weekends."

"That sounds so perfect for me," Dina said with a grin.

"Ok, if you like, we can change the options, so you only see bears?" Lauren offered.

"Yes, let's!" Lauren took the phone, unticked several boxes and handed it back to Dina.

"You know, I think I really liked the very first bear-guy we saw, you know, the one with black hair and brown eyes. I felt an instant connection when I looked at his photo. How can we find him again?"

"Umm, we'll have to search for him," Lauren said regretfully. "The first three profiles the app showed you were just a teaser to get you interested, so his profile could be anywhere on the site."

"Damnit! It's going to be such a hard job scrolling though all these sexy bear shifters to look for him," Dina said, with a glint in her eye. Lauren picked up the bottle of wine.

"Well it looks like we're all out of wine, so how about I leave you to your search, while I go down to the store and get us another bottle?"

"Sounds like a great plan!" Dina said. "Let's order pizza too!"

"Definitely, girl! You know what I like," Lauren said, picking up her purse and skipping out of the apartment.

Dina ordered a meat feast supreme with extra jalapeños, and a quattro formaggio, and returned to scrolling. She was almost going cross-eyed from the parade of insanely hot guys being presented to her, one after another, and she was worried that she'd miss the one she was looking for, lost among so many other sexy man-bears. But, suddenly – there he was!

"My goodness!" she exclaimed. Her soft pink lips curled into a smile as she stared at his photo. There was no way she could've missed him. He had those deep brown eyes, like dark pools you could get lost in, and his goatee was so sexy. She had a real weakness for light beards; there was something so rugged and masculine about them. His body was something else. His chest was broad and deep, with well-developed pecs, and his arms were strong and meaty. He had nice abs, but he looked like a guy who really enjoyed his food, rather than a scrawny gym bunny. His skin was deeply tanned, and he had a sexy scattering of hair, beginning on his chest, and running all the way down to the top button of his faded blue jeans. His hip bones were just visible, and he had a red lumberjack shirt tied around his waist. Dina read his profile, her excitement growing by the second. It said he worked as a wood carver and volunteer firefighter; he lived out by the national park; he loved eating out, cooking at home, hiking, and playing with his two nephews. He'd love to meet a tall, voluptuous woman, with an adventurous spirit and a love of life. She could hardly restrain herself from getting up and bouncing around the room. *He was just too perfect!* At the bottom of his profile was a pink heart. *What does this mean?* She muttered, tapping it at the same time. As before, the graphic popped to reveal the message: *Want to find out if we're a match?* Without hesitating for even a second, she tapped the happy face icon.

At that moment, Lauren hurtled back into the apartment with the wine.

"You're not going to believe what's happened!" Dina exclaimed. Lauren opened the wine in the kitchen and brought it through to the living room.

"What?" she said.

"The bear guy's contacted me already!"

"Let me see!" Lauren snatched the phone out of her hand. "Oh my god, he messaged you within ten minutes of us completing your profile. Let's see what he said:

Hi, there. This is the first time I've messaged anyone on the app, but when I saw you, I knew I couldn't let you pass by. You're so beautiful, and you seem so genuine and good-hearted. But it wasn't just that: I felt such a strong connection when I looked at your profile, that I'm desperate to find out if we're fated to be together.

Hoping to hear from you,

Logan.

"Wow!" Dina breathed.

"He felt the same connection with you! This is awesome," Lauren said. "Shifters have destined mates, like, *the one* they're supposed to meet, and they devote their lives to finding them. It sounds like you might be his!" Dina's tummy tingled with excitement.

"But how is that possible?"

"No-one knows how. It's just the way it happens," Lauren said, but the end of her sentence was drowned out by the doorbell ringing. "I'll get it," she said, and headed downstairs again to pick up the pizza.

Dina stared at the guy's photo, thinking of what she was going to say to him. This was all so crazy. He wasn't playing it cool, like she expected guys to, and she felt like she owed him the same directness. While she was deliberating, she decided to see what he looked like as a bear again. She placed her thumb over his photo and swiped to the right.

"Huh?" she muttered. Instead of a photo of a bear, she was looking at the main list of profiles again. *What have I done? I must have slipped off his profile somehow.* She scrolled up and down, searching for it.

"These pizzas smell A-mazing!" Lauren yelled, coming

through the door. She deposited them on the coffee table, opened both boxes, grabbed a piece, and immediately began eating. After a couple of seconds, she glanced at Dina.

"What's the matter, honey? Why aren't you eating?"

"Oh, I don't know. I lost the bear-guy's profile somehow."

"What? What did you do?" Lauren shuffled closer, still chewing.

"I just wanted to see him as a bear again, so I swiped his photo, and he disappeared."

"You swiped that way?"

"Yeah."

"That's *right*, honey. That's what you do when you don't want to see someone's profile again." Dina's mouth fell open.

"I *did* swipe right! My gosh! I'm such an idiot! What do I do to get him back? Tell me quick!"

"Oh, god!" Lauren said. She ate the final bite of the first slice of pizza and wiped her hands on a napkin.

"Go ahead and eat. I'll try to figure it out," she said, snatching the phone from Dina's fingers.

"I can't find him," she said, ten minutes later. "That's how this app works. Swipe right and they're gone for good."

"No! Me and my clumsy fingers! Dina said with a groan." How could I have been so dumb?"

"Hey, stop," Lauren said. "It's an easy mistake to make, especially for someone who's not used to using apps. I shouldn't have let you loose on it without supervision."

"I have to find him, Lauren! There has to be a way! I'm serious.

This guy is so hot, and he's interested in me, and we might even be destined to be together. Not that I'm sure that I believe in this whole destiny concept. And now he's going to think that I don't even like him!" Dina's voice was becoming tight and panicky.

"Calm down, honey," Lauren said, squeezing her shoulder. "There'll be a way to find him. I'll send Tamika a message, describing him, and hopefully she'll know who he is, and then she'll be able to put you in touch with him."

"Really?" Dina said, eyes shining with hope. "Do you think that'll work?"

"With a bit of luck," Lauren said, licking her fingers. By now, they'd demolished both pizzas. She quickly typed out a message to Tamika on her phone, then flung herself back on the sofa with her glass of wine. "Now let's chill, and check out some more of these sexy shifters."

"I think I've made my choice already," Dina said.

"But you don't know for sure that you're going to be compatible. And it would be a shame to limit yourself in the meantime," Lauren said.

They looked through another 20 or 30 bear-shifter profiles. They were all gorgeous, but, for Dina, none of them matched up to the first guy. Then they went through her alerts. There were 15 different shifters wanting to find out if they could be a match for her.

"I don't know about some of these guys," Dina said. "But I have to admit, it's doing plenty for my self-confidence!"

"That's my girl," Lauren said. Dina went through and said no *thanks* to the non-bear shifters. She had set her heart on a big, furry guy, and that was all she wanted right now. Two alerts remained– one from a blond guy who was a polar-bear shifter, and one from a grizzly-bear shifter.

"Click on the alerts and look at the messages they've sent you!" Lauren said excitedly. Dina's finger hovered over them.

"I feel like I really want to wait and see if Tamika can find the first guy for me. I just have to know first," she said. "Can I wait to reply to the alerts?"

"Of course," Lauren said. If they think you might be their fated mate, they'll wait for as long as it takes."

Lauren was starting to yawn.

"Home-time for me," she said. "I've got a sleepy bear waiting for me in bed. I'll let you know what Tamika says as soon as I hear from her."

"Thank you so much for tonight," Dina said. "Goodnight, hun." They hugged each other, and Dina waved Lauren goodbye at the door. She stood on the doorstep, watching Lauren's retreating figure until she was out of sight. She was envious that her friend was going home to a big sexy man who'd take care of her. Normally her envy would have been a sharp, bitter pain deep in her stomach, a gnawing fear that she'd never find the right guy for herself. But tonight she had a sliver of hope that there could be someone out there for her. She brushed her teeth and climbed in between clean sheets, and fell asleep dreaming of a black-haired, muscular man with the most delicious deep brown eyes.

CHAPTER 2

Dina was on her way to work next morning when Lauren called.

"Good morning!" she trilled. Dina flinched at the volume of her voice.

"Good morning yourself," she mumbled, barely awake yet. Morning was definitely not her favorite time of day.

"Hun, I have the best news for you! You're going to be so excited!" Dina became marginally more awake.

"What is it?" she asked.

"So, I heard back from Tamika already. Unfortunately, she doesn't know who the guy is. She says he sounds like half the bear shifters on the app. I told her he was way hotter and cooler, but it didn't help. BUT! – this is the exciting part – it turns out she's been thinking about organizing a summer garden party to celebrate the two-year anniversary of the app, and my message was the motivation she needed to go ahead with it. She's going to invite everybody who has a profile on the app. So, with a little luck, your man will be there, and you can meet each other in the flesh!"

"That will be amazing!" Dina said. "So when's the party?"

"Next Saturday night."

"Wow, that's not a lot of time to find a new dress. But I guess I can go shopping this weekend. You'll come to the party too, right?"

"Of course, hun. You know I'm always there for you. I'll help you sniff him out. And you know I love a good party!" Lauren said. Dina broke into a grin.

"Thanks, Lauren. I'd be so nervous going by myself!" she said.

On Saturday, Dina and Lauren went shopping with their two other best friends, Melissa and Kristin. Luckily, the Hope Valley annual summer ball was being held the week after the Shiftr ball, so they all needed to get dresses anyway. Dina was bursting to tell Melissa and Kristin about the dating app and the guy she'd found, but she understood that she was sworn to secrecy. They were both single girls, and she thought they'd be perfect for the site too. She hoped that she'd find herself a shifter, not only for her own happiness, but so she could let one of them into the secret as well.

"I can't tell you how hard it was keeping my secret from you all that time," Lauren told Dina, when they were walking a distance behind the other two. "Every time you told me that you were lonely, or that you thought you'd never find a man, I was bursting to show you the app. So when I got together with Connor, it was like a double celebration!" Dina grinned at her friend's soft heart.

"I don't want to jinx it by saying anything," she whispered. "But I'm really hoping the same for Melissa and Kristin."

THE GIRLS ENJOYED a long day of shopping together, breaking often for coffee, then lunch, then more coffee, then happy-hour drinks. None of them enjoyed shopping for clothes, hating the discomfort of fitting rooms, and the way that dresses hardly ever fit them perfectly. But they managed to find a compromise by layering the shopping with lots of fun activities in between.

They'd collectively banned each other from wearing black, since it was a summer party, and had all picked out beautiful, flattering floral designs. Dina chose a chiffon dress in the palest mint green, with huge, cobalt-blue flowers on it. It had a tight waist, which showed off her hour-glass curves, a flowing ankle-length skirt, and a low, v-neckline that made the most of her bust. Lauren picked out a fuchsia-pink dress in raw silk, embossed with a lighter pink orchid design, cap sleeves and a raised, belted waist. Melissa chose a sleeveless, cotton knee-length-dress, which was white all over, except for a deep pink and yellow floral and butterfly pattern around the hem, while Kristin bought a sky-blue silk dress, cut high on the thigh to show off her height and great legs. Dina had watched the girls trying on one dress after another, all day long, and she thought they all looked amazing. At 5'1, Melissa was the shortest of the four of them, and the cut of the dress made the most of her curves, without swamping her. She had dark blonde hair, and cornflower blue eyes, and a slightly vacant expression that belied her fierce intelligence. Kristin was only an inch shorter than Dina, and she carried herself proudly. She used to play basketball at college, and she had an athlete's elegance, but she struggled with her weight due to PCOS. Out of the four of them, she probably had the hardest time accepting her curves, but only her closest friends knew it. To everyone else, she looked like a fearless, sexy woman.

WHEN THEY WERE DONE with shopping for the day, they went to Valentina's, their favorite cocktail bar, for early evening drinks. The other three seemed happy with their purchases. Dina was a little nervous about her dress. She often picked bold colors, hence the red number that featured on her Shiftr profile, but tended to stick with classic, understated styles, so this was something new for her. When she'd seen the dress in the store, she'd had a fantasy of herself as a fairy princess, floating around the garden party, looking mysterious and ethereal. But now she wondered if it would just look stupid.

"Not at all," the girls chorused when she voiced her doubts.

"You look so elegant, and delicate," Melissa said. Dina snorted. She could count on the fingers of one hand the number of times someone had called her delicate, and that was all before she'd turned 12.

"That dress is attention-grabbing, in all the right ways," Kristin assured her.

One cocktail turned into two, and then three, as the girls chatted excitedly about the upcoming party. Dina was joining in too, but her thoughts were all about next weekend's Shiftr party. Lauren flashed her conspiratorial glances when the others weren't looking, knowing exactly what was on her mind.

"Let's hope there'll be some hot guys there!" Lauren said. "They won't know what's hit them when you ladies walk in!"

"Honey, there are *no* hot guys in Hope Valley. I think we've established that," Kristin said drily.

"Hey, things change. People move to other towns."

"Uh huh. And in Hope Valley, everyone knows there's someone new in town before they've even had time to empty out their U-Haul. Trust me, *no* eligible bachelors have arrived in town in the past several months!" Kristin continued.

"Well, people also come to the summer party from towns all over the county," Lauren said. "It's become quite a big deal in recent years."

"Lauren, you're a sweetheart, and I know you're trying hard for us because you're all loved up with Connor, but I'm not expecting to meet anyone there," Melissa said, patting Lauren's hand. "I feel like my marriage was my one shot at lasting happiness. It didn't work out, after our stillbirth broke us up. I think I'm destined to be alone now, and I'm ok with that." Dina glanced at Lauren, who shot her a look of exasperation. Dina grinned, painfully aware that she'd be saying the same type of thing if she didn't have the Shiftr party to be excited about.

"I just want someone decent, you know," Kristin said,

breaking through a pause in the conversation. "I'm about ready to settle now."

"No!" Lauren almost shouted. "You deserve someone as amazing as you are!"

"Babe, the chances of me being able to have kids is very small. If I can find a guy who doesn't mind being childless, and is not a total slob, and treats me decently, well, maybe that's all I've got a right to expect."

"Ladies! Where did this lack-of-self-esteem avalanche come from?" Lauren said, looking appalled. "I thought me finding Connor would give you all hope that there are great guys out there. Now, no-one is going to settle or be an eternal spinster. We're going to go to the ball, all looking amazing, and we're going to have fun, and chat to lots of men. And I'm certain that, within six months, you're all going to be with someone incredible. And I don't want to hear any more negativity from any of you!" With that, she stalked over to the bar to get another drink.

The following week passed in a blur for Dina. She snuck onto the app a couple of times, checking her alerts. Each day, there were at least three more guys wanting to know if she could be their perfect match, but she was determined to hold off on replying before she'd been to the garden party. The sexy bear shifter was on her mind more often than not. The thought of his hot, naked torso turned her mind to mush. While she was teaching her elementary school classes, her mind was far away, concocting all kinds of fantasies about the things they could get up to together. Her ex-boyfriend hadn't been very adventurous in bed, which had been a constant frustration to her. She was a red-blooded woman, with strong appetites and urges, and the sex drought she'd suffered since Trey dumped her had driven her half-crazy. She loved the thought of being dominated in bed; of being overpowered by a really big, strong guy, who was capable of pinning both her wrists in one hand, while he pleasured every part of her body. When she lay in bed alone, she imagined the bear-guy doing exactly this to her – holding her down and taking her roughly, while he gazed at her with those dark, fathomless pools of eyes.

Although she'd only seen his photo for a moment, his image was burned into her brain. It was weird – she usually had to meet someone a few times before she could recall every feature of their face. But she remembered him as if she knew him intimately. And she had the strangest sense that those brown eyes were calling to her, across space and time. She pictured them as tender and insistent, telling her that she was the one. But as she tossed and turned, unable to sleep, the thought gnawed at her that he would have thought she'd rejected him, and already gone onto someone else.

"Relax, Little Miss Stresshead!" Lauren said, answering Dina's early morning call after one of those anxiety-ridden nights. "Even if he has started dating someone else, if you're the one, it won't matter. You'll be his destined mate."

SATURDAY CAME, and Lauren came over to Dina's place to get ready for the garden party. They ate a bowl of pasta each.

"I know what you're like – drinking too fast when you're

nervous – so we've got to line our stomachs first!" Lauren said. "Otherwise, Connor will be putting you over his shoulder and carrying you home before the party's even started!"

"You're right," Dina said with a giggle, recalling all the times she'd got way, way too drunk at parties in an attempt to hide her nerves, and then ruined any chance of meeting a guy there. "But I think I've learned to pace myself now I'm in my thirties!" Lauren cocked an eyebrow.

"Let's hope so, girl," she said.

After they'd finished eating, they began to get ready. They put on some music to get them in a party mood, alternating between Lauren's R'n'B favorites, and Dina's taste in light rock. Dina rubbed camellia moisturizer all over her body, making her skin impossibly soft and smooth, and then she put on a matching lacy lingerie set, in the same mint-green shade as her dress. It was beautiful and expensive, and she'd bought it during the week to give her an extra confidence boost. She slipped her dress on over the top. She still wasn't sure about the long, floaty skirt, but she did love the way it flared over her hips, and the nipped in waist. Her bra gave her boobs a nice lift, and the low v-neckline of the dress made her cleavage look amazing. She draped her favorite wrap over her shoulders. It had belonged to her grandmother, and was made of cream filigree lace.

She joined Lauren in the bathroom to do her make-up.

"You look stunning!" Lauren said, looking at Dina's reflection in the mirror as she applied her eyeliner.

"You're looking pretty hot yourself," Dina said, eyeing her friend's voluptuous figure in her tight pink dress. Lauren loved her curvy body and it showed; she always looked sensational.

Dina applied black liner and smoky gray eye shadow to her eyelids, to emphasize the greenness of her eyes. She added mascara, then picked up her favourite lipcolor and hesitated.

"Lipstick or not?" she asked.

"Not!" Lauren said. "You'll scare any guys off who might be thinking about kissing you." Dina giggled.

"Fair point, I guess."

"How about this one?" Lauren said, picking up a pot of rose-pink gloss. "It's so pretty."

"Ok." Dina slicked it on. It made her lips look extra full, and she completed the effect with a rose cream blush.

"Perfect!" Lauren said, in admiration. "Your eyes look kind of wicked, but your cheeks and lips have this fresh, kind of innocent look. It's the ideal virgin/harlot combination!"

"Hey!" Dina exclaimed, and slapped her friend's ass playfully.

They both stepped into killer heels – Dina in nude patent courts, and Lauren in black patent sandals – and walked into the bedroom to see themselves in the full-length mirror.

"Wooh! We're two hot ladies," Lauren exclaimed. Dina looked at her reflection more shyly. She looked pretty ok, she allowed herself to think. Before she could object, Lauren snapped a selfie of them together. "The before shot," she said with a cackle. "Ok, let's have one drink before we go, so we don't go in cold." She pulled a small bottle of tequila out of her purse. "Do you have soda, and lime?"

"Yes!" Dina said, striding over to the kitchen. She mixed up two drinks with ice. "I actually feel quite classy right now," she commented, as they drank them sitting on high stools by the island in the kitchen.

"Well we princesses better call ourselves a carriage, if we don't want to be late," Lauren said, reaching for her phone, and tapping on a taxi app.

CHAPTER 3

The venue for the garden party was out in the hills, a 30-minute drive from downtown Hope Valley. As the taxi passed between two high, wrought iron gates and drove onto a private tree-lined avenue, Dina's mouth fell open.

"What is this place?" she said.

"I don't know," Lauren replied. "But the person who owns it sure seems to have a lot of money!" The avenue continued for maybe a quarter of a mile, before it swung to the left and a huge, elegant house came into view. The house was white, with three stories, and big marble columns on either side of the front door. It gleamed like a Grecian temple under the flawless blue sky. To the right of the house was a painted wooden sign, saying *'Secret garden party this way'*.

The girls stepped out of the taxi carefully, Dina catching up her loose skirt so it didn't get tangled in the door, and they walked towards the sign. They were now close enough to see that there was a pathway running alongside the house. Lauren looked at Dina, her eyes full of excitement.

"Are you ready?" she asked. Dina let out a long breath.

"As ready as I'll ever be," she said. They picked their way along the path, and when they reached the end, they stopped and stared at the amazing sight that greeted them.

There was a huge garden, full of palms and magnolia trees, with tables and chairs dotted here and there. A jazz band was playing in one corner, and in the other was a vast buffet table, groaning with food. Off to one side was a cocktail bar that looked like it had been lifted out of the 1920s, and in the final corner was a mini circus show, with acrobats and jugglers and fire-eaters. All the women were in pretty dresses, while the men were in tuxedos. Every guy that Dina glanced at was ridiculously, stunningly, good looking.

"Oh. My. God!" Dina breathed. "Is this place real?"

"Pinch me, I think I'm dreaming," Lauren said at the same time.

As they stepped onto the immaculately-clipped lawn, a man walked over with a tray of champagne glasses.

"Drink, ladies?" he asked. He had a narrow, handsome face, with something sly in his expression that made Dina think of a fox. Lauren snatched two glasses immediately.

"Thank you," she said.

"Are these men all shifters?" Dina whispered when the guy had walked away.

"Yup," Lauren replied, looking around. "And what fine specimens they are. Not that I'm looking, of course; Connor's all the man I'll ever need." As they walked into the center of the garden, they could hear the jazz band playing, and they were bathed in the sunlight of a beautiful summer's day. Dina tried not to stare too obviously at the men all around them, but she couldn't get her head around the fact that they were all half animal. And not only that, but they were insanely hot. She was practically salivating. Seeing such sexy men on the app had almost been too much for her; seeing them in the flesh was on a whole other level.

Just then, a woman in a shimmering golden dress ran over to them, tottering on incredibly high heels.

"Lauren, darling!" she exclaimed, taking Lauren by the shoulders and kissing her on both cheeks. "I'm so sorry I wasn't there to greet you at the entrance. I just got caught up with so many people!" She turned to Dina. "And you must be Dina." She also kissed Dina, while Dina stood there, too stunned to move. "I'm Tamika, and I'm so glad you've made it here tonight! Lauren told me all about that delicious man you found on Shiftr, and I can tell you that I'm pretty sure he's here tonight. All but two of the local shifters responded to my invite, saying they were coming."

"That's great," Dina said, a little shyly. Tamika's effervescent personality had knocked her off balance a little. She was a beautiful woman in her mid-forties, with long, caramel-colored hair, carefully arranged into waves, and long, muscular, tanned legs. Her dress was a simple shift style, but it looked stunning on her generous curves, and she wore bold, statement jewellery, set with jade stones. She spoke in a booming voice with a foreign accent. "Where are you from?" Dina blurted out.

"I'm from England, darling," Tamika said with a smile. "I grew up in London, but an American werewolf caught my heart ten years ago, and brought me over here. I've lived in the US ever since. Just recently, I started thinking about all the lonely shifters out there who are desperate to meet curvy girls like us, and the idea for the app just popped into my head!"

"It's amazing what you're doing," Dina said, gazing around the garden.

"Thank you, darling. I very much hope you find the bear you're looking for. Please come and find me if he hasn't emerged from the shadows by the end of the night!" Tamika said. And, with that, she was off, greeting the next group of people.

"She's quite something!" Dina whispered to Lauren.

"She is," Lauren replied with a grin. "I've heard that she belongs to the English aristocracy or something, and she's a millionaire, so she produces the app for free, just to bring curvy girls and shifters together."

"That's so sweet," Dina replied. "Oh, hey, isn't that Connor?" By the time she'd finished her sentence, the tall, stocky figure of Connor was right in front of them.

"Hey, baby!" Lauren yelled, throwing her arms around him. He kissed her on the lips, tenderly stroking the bare flesh of her upper arms. Dina was entranced. She loved the way Connor treated Lauren, like she was the only girl in the world. Eventually, they pulled away from each other, and Connor turned towards Dina with a big grin.

"Sorry, Dina, I forgot my manners! It's great to see you!" he said, and pulled her into a hug that almost knocked the breath out of her. Fleetingly, she wondered if that was how it would feel to be held by the bear-guy.

When he released her, she registered how handsome he looked in his crisp white shirt and bow tie. She was used to seeing him in a t-shirt and ripped jeans.

"How are you?" he asked her, a warm smile lighting his eyes.

"A little nervous," she admitted.

"Don't be. You're not going to have a hard time finding your mate, trust me," he said, squeezing her hand. "Now, would you ladies like to come over and meet my clan?" He nodded to an area of the garden where a group of well-built, dark-haired guys were gathered.

"Your clan?" Dina asked. Connor laughed.

"Sorry, I forget people aren't used to shifter language. It means something like my extended family." They walked over to the group together. On the way over, a waiter appeared at their elbow with a tray of delicious-looking canapés, and Dina and Lauren grabbed one each.

As they arrived, all eight men turned around to greet them, and Dina was shocked to see approval and desire in the eyes that lingered over her body.

"This is Ryzard, Olsen, Bruno, Dalton, Frankie, Leigh, Niall, and Timo," Connor said. "Guys, this is Dina." They sweetly shook hands with her, one at a time, and she felt herself blushing as she met their intense gazes. Connor frowned. "Someone's missing though. Where's Logie?"

"He's on a mission," Bruno said with a laugh. One edge of Connor's lips curled up.

"What kind of a mission?"

"He said he found this amazing woman on Shiftr," Frankie

cut in. "She seemed to like him too, but then she disappeared, and he couldn't find her on the site anymore."

"He's been really cut up about it all week, because he's sure they were perfect for each other. So he's desperately hoping she'll be at the party today," Ryzard explained.

"He says he'd never forgive himself if she was here and he didn't manage to find her," Dalton added. Dina was totally charmed by the way they spoke, each picking up where the other one left off. But there was another, far more dramatic thought racing through her mind. She shot a glance at Lauren and saw that she was thinking the same thing.

"What does this Logan look like?" Lauren asked. The bears looked at each other and rubbed the backs of their heads.

"Pretty much like us?" Niall mumbled, confused.

"I mean, does he have black hair, or brown? Is he tall or average? What color are his eyes?" Lauren said. They looked relieved.

"Black hair!" Timo said triumphantly. "And he's real tall, maybe the tallest out of all of us."

"And his eyes?" The bears shuffled around.

"We don't know," Connor said with a laugh. "It's a guy thing. I can tell you they're not blue, but apart from that, I wouldn't have a clue." He shrugged helplessly. "Why are you asking, anyway?"

"Oh, no reason," Lauren said. "Dina and I just need to use the little girls' room. Could you point us in the right direction, Connor?"

Lauren dragged Dina off to a quiet spot under a tree, far from the others.

"Did you hear that?" she hissed. "He's here! He's looking

for you! How amazing is that?" Dina looked excited and terrified all at the same time.

"What if he doesn't like me when he sees me?"

"Please! Girl, you've never looked prettier, and you look better in the flesh than in your photos anyway." Lauren put a finger on her lip. "Now, what should we do – should we wait for him to find you, or should we be a little more pro-active?"

They began to wander around the garden together, focusing their attention on any guy walking around by himself. Every guy they saw was either too blond, too short, or not stocky enough. Then, right on the opposite side of the garden from where Connor and his friends were gathered, there was a man with his back to them. He was about 40 feet away, and Dina could see that he was taller than most of the men there.

"Turn around," she muttered under her breath. Incredibly, as she spoke, he did turn his head, as if looking for something. Dina clutched Lauren's arm as he turned to face them.

"Oh my god, it's him!" she hissed. There he was. Black hair, a hint of a beard, and six foot five inches of dense muscle, packed into a sexy tux.

"Are you sure?" Lauren said. "I can't even make out his features from this far away."

"Yes. I'm sure," she said. The man's gaze focused in on her, and a dazzling smile broke across his rugged features. He strode across the grass, and in an instant, he was standing in front of them. His deep brown eyes locked with Dina's, and she restrained a gasp. He was absolutely gorgeous, but it was more than that: she had the weirdest sense that they were being magnetically drawn together. He took a step closer, and held out his hand. Dazed, she stretched out her hand too, and he engulfed it in his. His whole hand was rough and callused, and she found herself wondering how it would feel running all over her body.

"I'm Logan," he said, in a deep, rumbling voice that made her quiver from head to toe.

"Dina," she replied, her voice an octave higher than usual.

"We met briefly online," he said.

"I know," she replied, with a giggle. *Idiot*. She'd planned to come across as mysterious and sexy, but she was so stunned by his good looks that she was acting like a teenager. He frowned, as if uncertain how he should phrase his next sentence.

"You're even more beautiful than your photos. I appreciate that you think I'm not your type, which is why I couldn't find you on the app after you received my message. But when we first made contact, I felt so strongly that we were a match. When I saw your photo, it was like a bolt of electricity was connecting your phone with mine." He laughed, embarrassed. Then he paused, frowning adorably, before he began to speak again. "So I wanted to ask if you'd be willing to give it another chance. Maybe we could hang out today, and get to know each other a little?"

"It was a mistake – " Dina started to say, but she was cut off by Lauren giving a little scream.

"Oh my god, I'm such a klutz!" Lauren exclaimed. Dina's head snapped to the side, and she saw that her friend had spilled her drink down the front of her dress. "Goodness. I'd better go to the restroom and fix this," she said, grabbing Dina by the hand and beginning to run. "I'm sorry, Logan, it was nice to meet you. We'll catch you later!" she called over her shoulder.

"Oh no, you've ruined your dress," Dina said, as they reached the restroom.

"It'll be fine with a little water," Lauren said. She took a paper towel from the dispenser, moistened it under the faucet, and began dabbing at the stain with a napkin. "Honey, you've got to make Logan work a little for you. You can't let it come too easy. Let him woo you and seduce you. Guys need to feel like they've won you over somehow, and it's important for you to feel like they've made an effort." Dina gaped.

"You've spoiled your dress to tell me this?" Lauren looked a little embarrassed.

"Well, I could see you were steaming in there like a bull at a gate, and I had to hold you back somehow!" Dina laughed.

"But are you sure about this?"

"Trust me. Connor and I courted for a long time on the app before we ever met up, and then he took me out for some really romantic dates. The chase is half the fun of dating."

"Ok. I'll do what you say. You've never been wrong before. You're the best, Lauren," Dina said, and hugged her best friend tight.

Dina looked at her reflection in the mirror and applied more lip gloss and Lauren helped her primp her hair a little.

"Now go, and be romanced," Lauren said, eyes sparkling.

LOGAN HADN'T MOVED from the spot where they'd left him, but he was holding two fresh cocktail glasses. The sight of him, waiting for her, made Dina catch her breath. This time Lauren introduced herself to him properly, shaking his hand.

"I need to go catch up with my man now, so I'll leave you two to get acquainted," she said, and floated off. The front of her dress was still wet, but she managed to carry it off with total elegance.

Logan turned to Dina, and she suddenly felt weak and quivery at being alone with him. He had such a strong, powerful presence, and he towered over her, which was a delicious sensation. At her height, there weren't too many men who were capable of doing that.

"You look breathtaking," he said. "And your dress suites you so well. You remind me of a fairy, or a woodland pixie." Dina blushed, and bit her lip, forcing back the self-deprecating comment that was threatening to spill from her mouth.

"Thank you," she said instead. He held out both cocktail glasses.

"I took a chance on the drinks," he said. "This one's a Lavender Martini, and this is a Summer Negroni. Take your pick." Dina took the Martini from him.

"I love Martinis," she said, smiling up at him. Her eyes lingered on his full lips and his sexy, perfectly-trimmed goatee.

"I've heard there's another garden just behind this one. Would you like to go investigate it with me?" he asked.

"Sure, that sounds like fun!" They began to walk towards the rear of the garden, and Dina did feel a little like a fairy, floating along in her gauzy dress, tiny in comparison to this huge man.

At the edge of the garden, they passed through an archway, made of climbing roses entwined with vines, and they entered a second, completely different garden. A tall, manicured hedge stood directly in front of them, stretching all the way to the left and the right.

"Is this a maze?" Logan said, excitedly.

"I think it might be!" Dina said. "I used to love playing in mazes when I was a kid."

"Which way?"

"Let's try left," she said, and began walking. The path was narrow, just wide enough for them to walk side by side. At the end, it twisted around to the right, and then forked. They picked the right fork.

"Is your family from Hope Valley?" Logan asked her.

"Yes. For several generations. And I've never wanted to live anywhere else. I just love the feeling of community, the way that everyone knows everyone. I guess I'm a typical small-town girl," she finished, with a shrug. "How about you? I don't think you live downtown, or we would've met long ago." He laughed.

"No, I live out by the national park. There's a few of us there."

"The guys Connor introduced me to?"

"Yes! All the clan are together. I've lived near the park all my life, and my parents live on the opposite side of it now. It's nice to have a little distance from them, but I could never be too far away."

"Must be great to be out in nature all the time?" she said.

"It's a necessity for me. If I lived in the city, I think I'd wither away. I need to wake up and hear bird song, and smell the forest."

Dina glanced at him when he wasn't looking. She loved the way that he was so connected to the earth. It was fresh, and genuine.

"Have you been on Shiftr for long?" he asked hesitantly.

"Nope, I'm a newbie," she said. "Lauren talked me into joining after she met Connor through there."

"That's great," he said. "Connor and I joined at the same time, after Tamika hunted us down and told us how great it was. He found his match pretty quickly, but I'm still looking for mine. I mean, I was, until – " He broke off, and glanced at her. She looked up and met his gaze. The sun was shining full into his eyes, making his irises appear lighter than before, and she could make out the quick dilation of his pupil. "I know my profile isn't very good," he said. "It's so hard to write about yourself. I guess I felt kind of embarrassed, and it came out really lame."

"Oh, mine was terrible!" Dina said. "I had to have Lauren help me out with it."

"Well, the end result was worth it," he said. "I only got to see it for a minute, but I remember your photos, and how beautiful you looked in that red dress. And your eyes were so green and sparkly, just like they are now." At that moment, Dina stumbled in her heels on a large stone. Logan's hand shot out to steady her, curving around her waist.

"Are you ok?" he asked, eyes full of concern.

"I am now," she replied, with a smile.

Afterwards, he didn't remove his hand immediately, but let it linger on her hip. She could feel the heat from his fingers coming through the flimsy fabric of her dress, scorching her skin beneath. She also became aware of his scent – rich, spicy and outdoorsy. She didn't think it was cologne, but his own natural smell. She inhaled deeply, letting it fill her nostrils, and it hit her like a drug, making her feel hungry and full of desire for him. She was also weirdly conscious of the sound of his breathing. It was a very subtle undertone – a low rumbling sound, kind of like a cat's purr.

"I loved that you were into dancing and hiking," he continued. "Two things that I really enjoy in life."

"Yeah, I love to hike," Dina said. "I've always dreamed of doing one of those famous trails, like the Appalachian."

"Me too!" he said. "If you ever need a partner – " he trailed off, realizing what he was saying. Dina smiled to herself. There was something delightfully awkward about him, as if he wasn't used to dating.

"And you tutor kids too?" he said.

"Yes. I'm an elementary school teacher, and I also volunteer a couple of times a week at a local project to give vulnerable kids a little extra support. I've been doing it for a few years and I can see it makes a difference to these kids' lives."

"That's great," he said, eyes shining. "I really believe in supporting the younger generations too. I take on a couple of apprentices at my wood-carving business every year. They're shifters though, of course. It would be too difficult to hide our true nature from humans, day-in day-out."

"I'm surprised it's been kept a secret for so long," Dina said.

"Oh, it's been closely guarded for generations. There are some who are nervous that the app will ruin everything. But the truth is that there are a lot of lonely shifters out there, who don't have the skills to meet the right woman, and their species is dying out as a consequence." He stopped walking and looked at her very seriously.

"Dina, how do you feel about me being a bear?" he asked her. At his words, a bolt of heat hit her clit, and ran deep inside her. The truth was, she was beginning to find it very sexy.

"It was something new to me, of course," she stuttered. "But I actually really like it. I think it's nice." She looked up at him, into those smoldering chocolate eyes, and she couldn't hold back. "I think it's really hot," she said, at last. Logan's breathing became louder, a definite rumble, and he leaned towards her, his lips inches from hers. *He's going to kiss me!* she thought, at the same moment that he straightened up, and began walking again.

"Sorry," he mumbled.

"No, don't be – " she said awkwardly. Falling a step behind him, she shook her head. *Damnit. He still thinks I don't like him.* She gazed at his muscular back, his black jacket straining over his powerful shoulders. But nothing could be further from the truth.

As they'd been walking, the turns in the line of hedge had become more frequent, and they'd picked the directions subconsciously, lost in their conversation. They were now deep in the maze, and the tall, dark green hedges seemed to be crowding in on them. Dina might have felt uneasy if she'd been alone, but Logan made her feel safe, somehow, even though he was still a stranger to her. Another turn brought them to a small open area. There was a bench, with a canopy of vines arching above it, and in front was a tiny rose garden, and an ornate fountain, tinkling softly. They peered into the water. It was full of orange and white koi carp.

"I think we've found the center!" Logan said. It was a lovely spot. The red, pink and white roses were beautiful, and, as they walked closer, Dina could see that the vines were passionflowers – her favorites.

"This was so worth the walk," she said.

"Shall we take a rest here? It's nice to be in the shade for a while," he said.

"Sure." She sat down on the bench and took a sip from her drink. She'd been so caught up in Logan's presence that she'd forgotten to drink it. It had lost its chill by now, but the alcohol made her pleasantly lightheaded. Logan sat down too, leaving a small space between them. The scent of the passionflowers was intoxicating, but the smell of him was much stronger. It was a masculine, deeply exciting scent, and she longed to be close to him, smelling his neck, wrapped in his strong arms.

"I'm not surprised you rejected my profile, Dina. It was pretty poor. But I'm so, so glad that you've given me another chance to get to know you today," he said. Dina looked into his eyes, feeling giddy, almost hypnotized by the intensity of his gaze, and the nearness of his firm, full lips. She couldn't conceal the truth from him any longer.

"It was an accident," she said. "My clumsy thumb swiped in the wrong direction. I was trying to look at your bear photo again, but instead I deleted you from my list altogether." He broke into a grin, his straight, white teeth dazzling.

"Really?"

"Yes. Unfortunately I am that much of a doofus," she said, her cheeks warming.

"So the message I sent you didn't put you off? I was so happy when you said you wanted to find out if we were a match. Then, when you deleted me right after you saw my message, I was worried I'd come on too strong."

"Not at all," she said. "I thought it was beautiful. And I came here today because I was hoping I'd find you here."

He gave a deep rumble. Dina jumped.

"What was that?" she exclaimed.

"It was my bear," he said. "It's a sound of happiness."

"It does that every time you're happy?"

"Yes." he shrugged. "It's an instinctive reaction. Actually, I want to show you my bear now."

"You mean you're going to shift into a bear right here?" Dina said, caught between horror and fascination. Logan laughed and pulled his phone from his breast pocket.

"No, I was just planning on showing you the photo that you were looking for. If you still want to see it?"

"Of course!" Dina said. She watched as he opened the app, and located his profile. The screen filled with the photo of him that had initially drawn her to him so strongly. He swiped left, and a large bear filled the screen instead. She took the phone from him and looked closely at the photo. The bear was huge, with glossy black fur, dangerous-looking black claws, a long, blunt muzzle, and deep brown eyes. It was standing on its rear legs, its front legs up against a fir tree.

"He's beautiful," she said, knowing instinctively that Logan would appreciate a compliment on his bear side.

"One day you'll see me as a bear, if you'd like?" he said.

"I really would," she said, her voice a shade above a whisper. Unconsciously, they'd moved closer together to look at the photo, and his knee was now brushing against her thigh. He leaned towards her, hesitantly. She met his eyes, seeing that his pupils were dilated, and reached out and touched his chin. He edged still closer, and, as his face went out of focus, she closed her eyes and their lips met. His lips were impossibly soft, gliding on hers. She felt the warmth of his breath, and the softness of the stubble on his chin. He drew back, as if assessing her reaction, before planting another kiss on her lips, and then another. They were sweet, soft kisses that made her impatient for more. She made a small sound, and her lips parted under his. He began to kiss her more confidently, his lips caressing hers, sensitively, exquisitely. A spark of desire was ignited deep inside her, and when she felt the flickering touch of his tongue, the spark grew into an intense warmth, suffusing her body. She hadn't been kissed for so long that she'd almost forgotten what it felt like. In fact, she'd never had a kiss like this before. His lips were so soft and tender, making her dizzy with pleasure, and the touch of his tongue was velvety and exciting, as it danced into her mouth and seeking out hers. Logan's arms wrapped around her waist, pulling her closer to him, and she responded by clasping hers around his neck. From time to time, his stubble brushed her cheek, and she found herself wondering how it would feel brushing her tender inner thighs. His hand moved into her hair, his fingers getting caught up in the strands, measuring its weight.

"God, Dina, you feel so incredible," he muttered, drawing

away from her for a second. She rested her hands on his shoulders.

"No, you do, Logan," she replied, and she pulled him into another deep kiss. She'd had no idea that kissing could be so arousing. She was aware of her nipples, hard and aching beneath her lacy bra, and the growing ache between her thighs. She sensed that a part of her, which had been sleeping for too long, was finally waking up. She longed for him to touch her all over, wanted to feel those big rough hands caressing every part of her body. He was being the perfect gentleman though. While his kisses were becoming more and more intense, his tongue probing her mouth more and more urgently, his hands stayed on her waist, or her jaw, or her shoulders. When, at last, his hand moved down and touched her thigh, her flesh was so sensitized and eager for his touch that she jumped at the contact.

"Sorry," he muttered. "I think I was getting a little carried away." He looked around guiltily, as if worried that they were being watched. But they were still alone. "I feel like we've been kissing for hours. I've been so lost in you." She felt around in her purse and pulled her phone out.

"Well, it's almost six already, so that's definitely a possibility," she said with a grin. He cupped her face in his hands.

"I don't ever want to stop kissing you," he said, and fell on her lips again. She sensed the passion and hunger coiled tightly inside him, and was amazed that he managed to hold it in.

Suddenly, Dina's tummy rumbled, and they both laughed.

"God, I'm such a stupid bear. I've been keeping you out here all day without anything to eat or drink. Let's go and get some food," he said, getting to his feet and holding out his hand to her. Dina stood up, her hand naturally sliding into his. She *was* pretty hungry, now she came to think of it.

"Which way is it?" she said, aware that she had no idea of the turnings they'd taken to arrive in their secret spot.

"It's this way," Logan said, and walked confidently to the left. They passed through the maze quickly, never taking a wrong turning.

"But – how can you know this?" she said.

"I just followed our scent from earlier."

"That's amazing," she said. He shrugged.

"Just one of the advantages of being half-bear," he said. They held hands the whole way, and Dina tingled with happiness. She loved feeling so small and protected by him.

THEY RETURNED to the main garden just as the sun was setting. The sky was brilliant shades of yellow, salmon pink and orange. Little white lanterns at the edge of the lawn were flickering into life, and the scent of night flowers filtered into the air. As they strode across the lawn to the buffet table, many eyes turned in their direction. Dina felt self-conscious, but in a nice way, as if everyone was looking to see who was walking with this big, sexy man.

The buffet was the most delicious-looking that she'd ever seen. There was seafood – lobster, oysters, shrimp and mussels, sliders with all kinds of fillings, huge trays of roast meats, chicken wings, cold cuts, cheese, and trays of fries and onion rings. At the side was a chef cooking steaks fresh on a barbecue, and you could choose any cut you wanted. While

Logan lined up to have a steak cooked, Dina picked up a couple of sliders and a handful of fries. She was salivating at all the food, but she didn't want to seem unladylike by loading her plate up.

Logan came back with a giant t-bone steak, so big that it was overhanging the edges of the plate. He frowned at her plate in confusion.

"What's wrong? You were really hungry," he said. Dina stammered something vague.

"Ah, I get it, it's difficult to manage while you're holding your purse. Here." He passed his plate to Dina to hold. "You want some roast beef? Chicken wings?" As she nodded at this and that, he filled her plate up until it was as overloaded as his own. "That's better," he said in satisfaction. They looked around at the tables. "Do you want to go find Lauren?" Dina squinted. She could just make out her friend's pink dress in the distance.

"No, I think she's good hanging out with Connor," she said.

"I was hoping you'd say that," he said, looking at her with intensity. "I wanted to spend some more time with you alone."

They located a table for two, in a secluded spot at the edge of the garden. Now that it was almost dark, the sky deep navy, with a crescent moon showing, other lanterns came to life, and their little table was lit in a soft orange glow. There were tea lights on the table, and as soon as they sat down, a waiter appeared with a tray of champagne glasses. They took one each. When the waiter had walked away, Logan raised his glass.

"Here's to us meeting today, despite the obstacles that fell in our way," he said. Dina grinned and they clinked glasses. As she sipped the delicious cold champagne, she felt like she was in a dream. Things like this didn't happen to a girl like her.

Seeing how enthusiastically Logan dove into his food, Dina didn't hold back. It was so liberating being able to enjoy her food like this with a man. Her ex-boyfriend had always been picking at her, telling her what she should eat, making little digs about her weight. She'd come to terms with being a big girl. She knew she'd always be curvy, and she kept herself fit and healthy by hiking. But there was always that little voice niggling away, saying men wouldn't like her unless she starved herself.

Logan cut a hunk of his steak off and deposited it on her plate.

"You've gotta try this," he said. "It's almost as good as the meat the guys and I cook when we have our barbecues at home."

"Oh, I love barbecues," she said.

"It's a real bear thing. There's nothing our clan like to do more than hang out at one of our cabins with a fire going, plenty of beer, and barbecued meat – most of which we've caught ourselves." Dina glanced at him sideways. She was still getting used to the idea that he would do things like hunt his own food.

"That sounds really cool," she said.

"It is. And you're top of the invite list for our next one," he said with a grin.

They finished eating, and she delicately dabbed her lips with a napkin. Logan looked at her, the flame from the tea lights reflecting in his eyes, making his features seem softer than before.

"I hope this isn't an intrusive question," he said. "But I've been wondering all night how someone as lovely and beautiful as yourself could be single."

"Oh." She looked down, and fiddled with the stem of her champagne glass.

"I've overstepped the mark, haven't I? I'm such a clumsy bear sometimes." He laid his hand on hers, his eyes full of concern.

"No, it's not that. It's a really sweet compliment. The truth is, I've been single for a while. I had a long-term boyfriend, but he didn't treat me so well. And when he left me, it knocked my confidence a lot, so I haven't been ready for dating." Dina didn't know why she was telling him this, but something about him convinced her that he wouldn't judge her negatively. Logan's expression clouded over.

"I'd like to meet this guy who thought it was ok to mistreat you," he said, clenching his fist. "He'd be very sorry by the time I was done with him, I can tell you that."

"Hey, it's ok. It's far in the past," she said, anxious to pacify him. He caught sight of her expression.

"I'm sorry," he said. "We bears come on a little strong sometimes. "It's our protective nature."

"It's ok, I like it," she said, entwining her fingers with his.

"I feel like I always want to be there to protect you, Dina," he said. "I can see that you're a strong, independent woman, but I'd love to be able to take care of you too." Dina gazed at him wordlessly. They'd only met today, but he seemed to be talking about *forever*. With an average guy, that would be a sign to run away very quickly, but Lauren had said that shifters mate for life. And she felt the same. As little as she knew him, this rough-tender man already seemed to be part of her destiny.

"How do you feel about having children?" he asked her, breaking into her thoughts. "I mean, one day, far into the future."

"Well, I love kids. They're definitely part of my plan," she said.

"Me too. I can't wait to have cubs."

"Cubs?"

"That's what we call the children of bear shifters."

"*Cubs*," she repeated, trying out the word. "I like it. So, if a human and a bear shifter were to have children, they'd still be cubs? They'd be capable of shifting as well?"

"Cubs, yes, of course," he said with a grin. "As to whether they become shifters – yes they should be. As long as the human and the shifter are a perfect match." They stared at each other for a long moment, and then he leaned towards her and their lips met, in a gentle, slow kiss. It was as if the world was falling away from her, and time seemed to be poised, waiting for them. All she was aware of was the feeling of his lips on hers, his soft stubble brushing her chin.

After a long time, they pulled away, and gazed at each other in wonder, glowing with a sense that something had passed between them. Strains from the jazz band reached Dina's ears, and she turned her head to look at it. The musicians were gearing up, getting to their feet to play their instruments, and people were beginning to dance on the small platform in front of it.

"Shall we dance?" Logan asked her.

"Yes!" she said, a smile blooming on her lips. He took her hand again as they stood up from the table, and escorted her to the dance floor, like a gentleman from another age. The garden looked beautiful and magical, with strings of lights suspended from the trees. It was all impossibly romantic, and Dina shivered in delight.

The band was playing a song from long ago, a quick, lively number. Logan pulled her into his arms as they stepped onto the platform, and began to move. He was a great dancer, she realized immediately, amazingly light on his feet for such a big man. He was doing a specific step. Dina didn't know it, but with her experience and instinct for dance, she kept up with him, and they were soon spinning effortlessly around the space. Logan switched to another step as the music changed, and the musicians' eyes twinkled as they watched them dancing.

"Do you know the tango?" he asked her. She nodded. It was her favorite step. As the piece came to an end, he went over and spoke to one of the band, and the music changed completely, to a sensual Latin rhythm. They came together, and began to dance energetically. Dina knew the moves inside out, having practiced constantly during her teens, and she fell into the rhythm, Logan twirling her expertly, as if they'd danced together all their lives. It was easy to get lost in the passion of the dance, even with a partner you weren't attracted to, but with Logan, it was on a whole other level. It felt like a prelude to making love, their bodies so close, his thigh sliding between hers, his arms holding her up as if she was as light as a feather.

At the end of the piece, they stopped, breathless, and there was a small round of applause. Dina looked around in shock; she'd had no idea people had been watching them.

"Bravo!" the saxophone player called to them. Then he spoke to the band, and they began to play a much slower piece. Logan pulled Dina gently against his body. He held her right hand in his left, and his other arm looped around her waist. They were so close that she could feel the slow, steady beat of his heart. In her heels, she was tall enough to peep over his shoulder, but in bare feet, she would've been able to lay her head against his chest. She very much liked the thought of doing that. They swayed gently together, not moving much, just enjoying the closeness of each other's bodies.

"Dina, I love dancing with you," Logan murmured in her ear. "It feels so sensual."

"I love it too," she replied, lifting her chin to look into his eyes. He brought his mouth down to hers and kissed her again. Little by little, they edged over to the side of the platform, until they were back on the grass, out of the glare of the lights that were suspended over the dance floor. They began to kiss more passionately now, exploring each other's mouths as they had in the secret garden. Dina's arousal, which had temporarily yielded to softer, more romantic feelings, rose up again fiercely, and a sweet ache began to blossom between her thighs once more. Their bodies entwined as they kissed, craving ever-closer contact. As one of Logan's muscular thighs slid between hers and pressed up against her clit, the heat inside her became almost unbearable. She imagined him touching her there, doing more than touching her. If he didn't stop soon, she wasn't going to be able to control herself. She could feel that her nipples were erect, pushing at her bra and her flimsy dress, demanding attention, needing to be taken into his mouth. He wrapped his arms more and more tightly around her, nibbling at her neck, burying his face in her hair, and she could tell that he was growing hard, that his desire for her was as strong as hers for him. This knowledge drove up her arousal by several notches, and she felt her panties becoming damp. She yearned for him to take them off, along with her bra and her dress, and make love to her for hours.

At last, he drew back from their kiss, and gazed down at her, his eyes very dark and fierce.

"God, Dina, you're driving me crazy," he said, his voice rough with desire. "If we don't stop right now, I'm going to have to carry you off to my cabin, and I won't be responsible for my actions." She looked up at him, her eyes bright.

"Maybe I don't want you to stop," she said, softly, yet firmly. That had to be the understatement of the year. Every part of her being was begging for him to take her, to fill her, to make her lose herself. He looked at her very seriously.

"Dina, baby, I've never desired anyone the way I want you right now. But maybe we should take our time. I want to get to know you, to learn everything about you, to understand your thoughts and feelings and dreams and ambitions. To know what makes you happy and sad. I don't want you to think that I just want you for one thing." Dina bit her lip, her heart fluttering with happiness at his words.

"I want that too – " she said, but the end of her sentence was drowned out by a loud *Ooooh!* and lots of shrieks of excitement. They looked back at the party that they'd forgotten existed. The circus act had gathered in the center of the garden, and they were setting up Chinese lanterns. One lantern had been released already, and it was floating into the night sky. Logan and Dina watched as it climbed higher and higher, until it became invisible. The couple who'd let it go looked blissfully happy, grinning and kissing each other.

"I hope they made a wish," Logan said.

"I think they did," Dina replied, with a smile.

"Let's release one ourselves," Logan exclaimed. This was all the encouragement Dina needed, and she skipped over to the circus entertainers, pulling Logan along with her.

"What color?" a man in tiger face paint asked.

"Red," they said at the same time. The man selected a lantern, lit the flame and handed it to them. They stood facing each other, holding onto two sides each.

"To you, me, and our future," Logan whispered to Dina. She repeated his words and, together, they released the lantern.

Logan stood behind her, his arms around her waist, and they watched their lantern blowing into the velvety night, glowing red and leaving a fiery train in its wake. They kept their gaze on it, until it was a golden dot, no bigger than one of the stars. Dina let her weight fall against him, enjoying the sensation of being supported, and he nuzzled her hair.

"Part of me could stay like this forever," he murmured. She didn't need to ask what the other part of him wanted to do, as she could feel his hardness pressing against the cleft of her ass, driving her crazy.

Lauren and Connor joined the line of people waiting for a lantern, and Dina and Logan watched as they took their turn, full of happiness and excitement. When their lantern had become invisible too, Dina called to them, and they ran over.

"Hey! I haven't seen you guys all day," Lauren said. "Been having fun?"

"We certainly have," Logan replied. Dina flashed Lauren a secret smile, indicating how much she liked Logan.

"Connor and I are just going to set off a lantern, and then I think we're done for the day. So I'll say goodnight to you guys." Lauren stretched up to hug Logan, and squeezed her arms around Dina.

"Go get him, girl," she whispered. "Connor's been telling me all day how awesome he is, and I can tell you'll be *so* well suited!" Connor hugged Dina, and Logan and Connor exchanged some kind of complicated handshake, and a rough, back-slapping hug, and Lauren and Connor walked off together.

"How are you getting home?" Logan asked Dina.

"Oh, by taxi," she said.

"We could share, if you don't mind a slight detour by the national park?" Logan suggested.

"That would be great," Dina said, excited at the prospect of another half hour in his company.

As they walked out of the garden, Dina was a little regretful at leaving such a perfect, magical evening behind. There was a line of cars waiting in the driveway.

"Complimentary service, courtesy of Shiftr," the guy organizing the cars said as they walked up. "The driver will take you anywhere you want to go, just tell him your destination." They climbed into the luxurious sedan, and it pulled away from the house, tires crunching on the gravel.

CHAPTER 4

Dina and Logan sat close together on the car's soft leather seats. Logan clasped her hand, letting the back of his hand rest on her thigh. The contact with his body was almost unbearable. She longed to unfasten her seatbelt and jump on top of him. Instead they sat calmly, chatting about their lives. He seemed to want to know the smallest details about her, asking her all about her family and her friends, her job, and where she lived. She answered all of his questions, but her mind was wandering, thinking about how hot his body had looked in his Shiftr photo, how much she wanted to see it in the flesh. Her mind constructed mini fantasies: him on top of her, thrusting inside her, his strong hands spreading her thighs.

She was so engrossed by him that she hadn't noticed that the road had become a lot darker, the streetlights further apart. She'd been to the national park plenty of times before, but she didn't recognize this road. Logan leaned forward to direct the driver, and the car took a sharp turn, and the road became a rough track.

"Funny, I don't know this part," she said.

"There's a reason for that," Logan said, his white teeth flashing in the dark. "We were-bears need our privacy from the human world, if we're going to keep our existence a secret." He spoke to the driver again, and the car made another turn, then came to a stop at the side of the road, beside a gap in a line of trees.

"Where's your place?" she said, confused.

"Through the trees, a hundred yards back," he said. "Some of the other guys and I have cabins back there."

"That sounds really nice," she said.

"It's the best," he said with a grin. He unfastened his seatbelt and turned to her. "It's so hard for me to leave you here, so I'm going to kiss you goodnight quickly and go, before I lose all self-control." His lips brushed hers, and he opened the car door. "Good night, beautiful," he whispered. He climbed out of the car and closed the door. The driver began to pull away, and Dina watched as Logan strode into the dark woods. His kiss was still burning on her lips, and there was an unbearable ache between her thighs. But even more than that, she felt a hole, a vast emptiness in her heart, at being separated from him.

"Stop!" she yelled. The driver jumped and stepped hard on the brake.

"Sorry, ma'am?" he said.

"Hold on, I've made a mistake!" she said. She unfastened

the seatbelt, and scrambled out of the car. She ran back to the clearing and stared into the woods, but she could no longer see anything.

"Logan!" she yelled.

"Dina?" came a voice from far away. A second later, she saw a flash of his white shirt and he came crashing back.

"What is it?" he said, panicked.

"Logan, take me home with you," she said simply.

"Dina, if you come in here now, you're not going to leave for several days. I hope you realize that," he said.

"It's a good thing there's vacation from school next week," she said, coquettishly. His face broke into the most beautiful smile she'd ever seen. He bounded over to the taxi and told the driver that she didn't need a ride anymore, then he took her hand.

"Wait," she said, as she began to stumble into the undergrowth in her heels. Logan paused and looked down at her feet.

"Oh, sorry," he said with a laugh. With no hesitation, he bent down, swept her up, and strode off with her into the woods. Dina lolled in his arms in a daze; she hadn't been carried since she was a small child, and she hadn't thought it was possible to feel so small and vulnerable again. He looked at her tenderly as he walked.

"It's just a little bit further," he said, his breath a soft rumble. The woods looked entirely black to Dina. The meager light cast by the crescent moon left the night very dark, and she couldn't see the trees at all, but Logan navigated the track with ease.

At last she could make out a row of cabins. Each had a small light above the door.

"This is mine," Logan said stopping at the third one along. Three steps led up to a small veranda and a covered porch with an arched roof. Still managing to hold her up somehow, he rooted in his pocket for his keys and unlocked the door. Dina made to climb down, but Logan held onto her.

"No, I'm carrying you over this threshold, baby," he said. Ensuring that she didn't bump her head on anything, he brought her into the cabin, and gently laid her on the sofa. Then he flicked a light on. Dina looked around. It was way bigger than she'd imagined from the outside. The living room was spacious yet cozy, with rustic wooden furniture, a huge, antique-looking leather sofa, and homely rugs and animal skins spread across the floor. There was a big open fireplace, loaded up with logs for a colder evening. Lamps in the corners cast the room in a subtle orange glow. Logan sat down next to her, and she immediately fastened her lips onto his, kissing him more passionately than before. Her hands ran all over his broad shoulders, his huge biceps, and felt for his pecs beneath his shirt. He drew back, looking at her with wonder.

"Dina, we don't have to do anything tonight. You can have my bed and I'll sleep on the sofa," he said.

"Logan, maybe it isn't obvious, but I want you. I want you real bad," she said, looking back at him with smoldering eyes. He hesitated for half a second, before throwing himself on her. He pushed her back against the sofa, and kissed her hard, his stubble chafing her skin, and his fingers tangling in her hair. He scooped her up and pulled her onto his lap, and as soon as her thigh made contact with his crotch, she felt his hardness, his need for her. His hands ran over her upper arms, into the v of her cleavage. Dizzy, drunk with desire, she swept her skirt up above her knees, turned to face him and straddled him. Now the bulge of his cock pressed right on that hot, aching place between her thighs, and a small sound escaped her lips. Logan's hands hovered around her ass, as if uncertain whether he could touch her there, but as she pressed herself closer to him, his fingers sank into her flesh, pulling her close, inciting her to grind against him. His tongue snaked into her mouth, seeking out hers, circling it, with an insistent, hungry motion. She matched his urgency, sucking on his lips, lashing his tongue with her own. Dina had never felt so hungry, so unashamedly wanton before. He kissed and bit her neck, from one side to the other. They pulled at each other's clothes, eager for skin-on-skin contact. She fumbled at his bow tie, eventually getting it unclipped, and threw it aside. Then, she opened the first four buttons on his shirt, wanting to get at his muscular chest. His skin felt unexpectedly soft beneath her fingers, as did his sprinkling of chest hair, and his muscles rippled. She needed more. Sitting back to give herself enough space, she opened his shirt all the way down. He pulled off his jacket, then his shirt, and she finally saw him, just the way he'd been in the photo. She ran her hands all over his upper body. She'd never touched big muscles before, and the feeling of the bulges and undulations was amazing.

"Your turn," he growled, his voice harsh with desire. His

hand went to the zipper at the back of her dress, and he pulled it all the way down, in a single motion. Gently, he eased the broad straps from her shoulders, and the entire front of the dress fell down, revealing her mint-green lace bra.

"Beautiful," he murmured, bending his head to the sensitive skin of her décolletage. He made a trail of kisses along her collarbones, and down, into the valley of her cleavage. Hesitantly at first, and then more hungrily, he cupped her breasts in his hands. As soon as his thumbs grazed her nipples, they became twice as erect, begging to be taken into his mouth. His fingers hooked into the top of the lace cup, and he dragged it down, freeing her nipple. Dina watched as he brought his mouth to it, flicking his tongue over the tip, before fastening his lips around it. He sucked gently, and the sensation shot a burning path down to her clit. Hardly aware of what she was doing, she rubbed herself back and forth against his bulging, rock-hard crotch, every movement drawing waves of tingling heat. He pulled down the other cup of her bra and gave her other nipple the same treatment. With one breast in his mouth, and the other cupped in his strong hand, she was ready to combust with need. She could tell she was drenched, and she was probably leaving a wet mark on his pants, but she didn't care. She needed him inside her so badly.

He went to unfasten her bra, but then he paused and looked up at her.

"Let's do this properly," he said. "I want to take you to bed, and treat you like the goddess you are."

"Ok," she said, looking at him in delight. He rearranged

her bra straps, and she climbed off his lap and got to her feet awkwardly. Her dress slid to the floor and she stepped out of it. She was still wearing her heels. She shrugged to herself. They'd come off at some point. His gaze swept over her body, his eyes full of fire. He led her to the back of the living room and through a doorway. There was a short passageway, with two doors leading off it. He opened the right hand door, and took her into his bedroom. It was just as cozy as the living room, with bare wooden walls and a huge bed. The head and foot boards were made of intricately carved dark brown wood.

That was all Dina had time to observe before Logan took hold of her again. His hands moved frantically all over her waist, back and breasts, while he alternately nibbled at her neck and gave her hard, biting kisses on the lips, which left them tingling. He backed her onto the bed, until she was sitting down. Standing before her, he unfastened his pants and tugged them off. He was wearing snug, black undershorts, the kind she liked best, and the bulge of his erection was huge. His thighs were bulky and muscular, and covered with dark hair. He knelt down between her legs, holding each calf tenderly in his hand as he slipped her shoes off. She loved the way he was forcing himself to be gentle with her, although he was obviously half-crazed with desire.

He lifted her up, laid her down, so she was lying fully flat on the bed, and then he arched over her, his eyes darker than ever. His brow suddenly furrowed.

"What is it?" she asked in alarm.

"It's my bear," he said. "It's driving me on to mate with you, and claim you as my own."

"It is?" she said, intrigued.

"It's so hard to hold it back," he said in a frustrated tone.

"But you don't have to hold it back."

"I do, Dina," he said. "I want to take my time with you. Get to know every inch of your body." She wriggled happily. No-one had said that to her before.

He let his weight come down on top of her, and she gasped at the sensation of full body contact. He wrapped his arms around her and kissed her deeply again. She curled her legs around his, drawing him closer to her, and their bodies seemed to meld into one, sliding together as if they were made for each other. Underneath her back, he reached for the clasp on her bra, and she arched to allow him to get at it. Slowly, reverently, he slid the straps off her shoulders, and lifted the bra off completely, exposing her large breasts, and swollen, aching nipples to his gaze. With a soft growl, he fell on them again, sucking harder than before, taking more of her breast into his mouth. She moaned, and lifted her thighs, wrapping her legs around his waist. He gave a deeper growl and his pelvis gave little jerks.

She groaned in frustration. She loved what he was doing to her nipples, but it was still a big tease. More than anything, she wanted their underwear to be cast aside, and him to be inside her. Suddenly, she raked his back with her nails. He stopped kissing her and sat up, a sexy smirk playing on his lips.

"I think you're taking on some of the energy of my bear," he said.

"Maybe I am," she said, a wicked grin lighting her face.

"But there's no rush is there?"

"No rush," she muttered, gazing at his torso. She did enjoy lying back on the pillow and drinking in the sight of this gorgeous man who seemed to be crazy about her.

"Good," he said, in a growly voice, and cupped her breasts in his hands as he leaned forward and planted a kiss between them. He began to knead at them, rolling her nipples between finger and thumb, as he licked a slow trail down her body, all the way to her belly button. His tongue circled it and flicked inside, and she sighed. She hadn't realized it was such a sensitive spot, but it seemed to have a direct connection with her clit, and she felt her little bud jolting as if sparks were flying off it. He continued on his way, licking and kissing her soft belly. She fought back a flicker of self-consciousness, then abandoned herself to the sensation. When he reached her panties, he tugged at them with his teeth. She was so enflamed with need, that even that small movement made her hips jerk. He kept pulling, until her neatly-trimmed, black triangle of hair was revealed. His nostrils flared, inhaling the scent of her, and he made a low rumbling purr. He hooked his fingers into the sides of her panties, and eased them over her hips. She raised her ass, and he slipped them all the way down, past her knees and ankles, leaving her completely bare.

"You're so beautiful," he said, returning his lips to the place he'd left off, and planted kisses all over her pubic hair.

"Such sexy fur," he muttered. She waited, dying for him to flick his tongue over her clit, but he took his time, moving over to the side, to the place where her belly met her upper thigh. He made a trail of kisses across the front of her leg, to her tender inner thighs, each kiss inflaming her like a line of fire ants. She jumped as he nibbled at the tender flesh there, moving higher, but maddeningly slowly. She closed her eyes, willing herself to stay calm. When his tongue finally made contact with her clit, she jumped as if she'd had an electric shock. To her relief, Logan gave up on teasing her, and latched on it, drawing it gently into his mouth. She moaned. As his lips sucked on it, his tongue made tiny back-and-forth motions across the tip. Before long, her breath began to come in pants, and her hands wandered down and tangled into his hair, keeping his head exactly where it was. He had an amazing technique, his rhythm never faltering, building and building on her arousal. He kept his hands on her thighs, her legs pinned to the bed, and she adored the situation of being held there and eaten out by the bear.

Her hips started to make little bucking motions – signs that an orgasm was near – and her grip on his hair became more aggressive. Little cries and moans escaped her lips, and he responded by sucking harder on her swollen little bud. At the edge of her vision, she could just make out that his ass was moving, as he rubbed himself on the bed, and the knowledge that licking her pussy was turning him on flipped her right over the edge.

"Oh my god, I'm coming!" she cried, as her clit spasmed under his tongue, and she exploded into a sharp, shuddering orgasm.

DINA COULDN'T MOVE for a long time afterwards. She let go of Logan's hair, realizing, to her embarrassment, that she'd been tugging on it the whole time. He lifted himself up, the muscles in his shoulders flexing, and climbed up her body, until he was face to face with her again.

"You taste like the sweetest honey," he whispered, caressing her cheek, and kissing her on the mouth. "You're so sexy, Dina. I could lick you all day." She tasted her own tangy sweetness on his lips, and she had an overwhelming urge to taste him too. She pulled at the waistband of his shorts, uselessly, since it was trapped between their bodies. He laughed.

"Ok, they're coming off," he said. "But I might not be capable of being gentle any longer."

"Good," she said, looking him right in the eye. "I don't want you to be." He gave a growl, reminding her of the animal inside him, and she shivered. She sat up and helped him to pull his underwear off, gasping when his cock was finally revealed. It was even bigger than she'd expected from the bulge in his underwear. It was bigger than the large vibrator she kept in her nightstand, and she'd always been a bit of a size queen when it came to her toys. She really enjoyed the feeling of being filled, but she wasn't sure if she could handle Logan's cock. He spread her thighs again and knelt between them, his thigh muscles bulging, and his cock looking like a dangerous tool.

"The moment I saw you on the app, I knew I wanted to mate with you," he said. "But I can hardly believe it's about to happen now."

"Me neither," she said. Every part of her being was tingling with anticipation, and it was all she could do to stop herself from jumping into his lap and impaling herself on his length.

He arched over her again, supporting his weight on one

arm, while he kissed her and slid his free hand up her inner thigh. She gave a little moan as he stroked her soft, damp hair, and ran his thumb between her sensitive labia. He circled her clit briefly, before slipping all the way down to her entrance. At the slightest touch, her pussy spasmed. This was exquisite torture. Slowly, achingly slowly, he slid his index finger inside her. Her nerve endings were so sensitized that it almost hurt. He moved in and out, and she squirmed. She needed more goddamnit! She glanced at his cock; it was just within reach. Her hand snaked out and she took hold of it with a firm grasp. Logan gasped, and his finger shot all the way in, his knuckles bumping at her entrance. A moment later, both his hands were on her thighs, spreading them further, and the tip of his cock was probing at her entrance. She took a deep breath as he eased himself inside her, her muscles resisting, then yielding to his girth. He kept his eyes on hers, and the look in them was wild and animal. It was a little scary for her, but deeply exciting as well. His length kept coming and coming, until with a growl, he went all the way in, his pelvis butting deliciously against her clit.

"Don't worry, I can take it," she whispered, sensing that he was restraining himself with a massive effort.

Something in him uncoiled, and he began to fuck her hard, vigorously. Back and forth, in and out he moved, in long, relentless strokes. Each thrust set her nerve endings on fire, and she yelped and moaned like a wild animal. Her pussy turned to molten heat, throbbing out of control. He lifted one leg over his shoulder and went even deeper, making her gasp, before she learned to accommodate him. He began to pound her like a jackhammer, and she loved it, crying out and digging her nails into his back. She wasn't a girl who liked to go slow. Fast, hard pumping was what drove her crazy. Before long, a second orgasm hit her, and her pussy spasmed hard around his cock.

"That feels so goddamn amazing," he said. "I love the way your pussy feels. So hot and tight." His dirty talk knocked her into a third orgasm, and a fourth, and she lay helpless, as wave after wave of pleasure hit her.

Suddenly, he sat up on his haunches, pulling her with him, and she balanced her weight on her knees and wrapped her arms around him as she rode his cock up and down. He gripped her ass with his hands, making her move to his rhythm. But she wanted it faster. Catching him off guard, she tipped him backwards, making him lie on his back, and without him slipping out of her, she switched to cowgirl style, riding him hard while she gazed down at his gorgeous body. He reached out and circled her clit with his thumb, and she came again and again. He let her take her pleasure until she was exhausted, and then he flipped her onto her back once more. They were so energetic together, she almost felt like they were wrestling.

Now her head dropped over the side of the bed, and she was helpless as he fucked her harder than ever before, holding her thighs flat and wide apart. She liked the feeling of being helpless, and the angle of his cock, rubbing against the front wall of her pussy.

Logan's breathing was rough, and all kinds of snarls and growls escaped him as he pounded her harder and faster. He paused to move her further down the bed, laying her head on a pillow, and then he held her close, gazing into her eyes.

"Dina, you're so beautiful, so incredible," he whispered over and over again. His movements became very quick and jerky, and, at last, he came, with a roar, his seed shooting deep inside her, suffusing her with heat.

They lay quietly for a long time, damp with perspiration, the smell of sex heavy in the air. Logan's face was nuzzled in Dina's neck, and the feeling of this big, sexy man lying between her legs was blissful.

"That was incredible, Dina," he said. "You're such a sexy woman. If I didn't know better, I'd think you had a tiger inside you."

"Was I too much?" she asked, instantly anxious that she'd scare him away. She felt like something long repressed had just been unleashed inside her.

"Not at all," he said. "You're the sex-mate of my dreams. We bears are very physical, and I've always hoped that my destined mate would be my match in terms of appetite and energy." Dina laughed.

"I think I've always had a huge appetite, but this is the first time I've met someone I've been able to indulge it with," she said. A look of delight came into his eyes.

"This is only the beginning," he whispered, running a fingertip over her face, exploring her cheekbones, her nose, her lips. "There's a lot more mating to come, trust me. Bears need to mate often, to maintain a deep connection with our mate. I need you to know that you're fully mine, and that I'm yours, your one and only, who will stay close to you and protect you to the ends of the earth."

"Logan, I would really like that," she replied. He held her and kissed her for a long time.

After a while, he got up and pulled the covers out from underneath them, then tenderly covered her body. She turned onto her side, and he snuggled against her, so that her face nestled into his chest. The last thing she remembered was him murmuring sweet compliments to her.

CHAPTER 5

The next morning, Dina awoke to the sight of Logan walking around the bedroom, butt-naked. He seemed to be looking for something, and she watched him drowsily, eyes half-open, so he didn't notice she was awake. He had such a hot, masculine body. There was nothing self-conscious or preening about him; he had real, human flesh on his muscles, and there were little scars on his body here and there. She cast appreciative eyes over his shoulders, his biceps, his pecs, his ass. She felt like she wanted to lick every inch of this sexy man. His cock was semi-hard, and the sight of it made her pussy muscles twitch. She thought about all the things he'd said to her last night, both about how much sex they were going to have in the future, and about how he wanted to be her permanent, life-long mate, and her belly warmed with happiness and desire all rolled into one. She gave a contented sigh, and Logan turned to look at her.

"Good morning, beautiful," he said, and walked over, climbed onto the bed next to her and enveloped her in a hug.

"Morning yourself," she said.

"How did you sleep?"

"Very well, I think. I didn't stir once."

"That's probably because it's so peaceful here." She listened, and all she could hear was the sound of birds.

"Maybe," she said, knowing it had more to do with the fact that Logan had been there. She didn't sleep well by herself, and last night, she'd fallen asleep feeling safe and protected, which was not a familiar feeling for her.

Logan pulled the covers back and climbed under them.

"Mmm, you smell so sweet," he said, nuzzling her. "Like acacia blossoms." His skin glided against hers as he held her against him. The touch of his body was instantly arousing, and Dina's mind started going wild with all of the things she wanted to do. She dipped her head and kissed him on the lips, reaching for his cock at the same time. He let out a groan, becoming hard in a second. She moved her hand up and down his shaft, with light, teasing strokes, and his hips gave little jerks. He tried to push her onto her back, but she put a hand on his chest and persuaded him to lay on his back instead.

"You know what I was thinking of doing just now, as I was watching you walking around?" she said.

"What?"

"Taking you in my mouth," she whispered. He made a sharp intake of breath, and, at the same moment, she ducked down and did just that. She licked all over the tip of his cock, teasing him, making light circles, moving up and down the shaft, until he was crazy with need.

"Dina, please," he whispered at last, and, finally, she positioned her lips over the tip and took his length into her mouth. He growled and snarled as she moved up and down, sucking him deeper and deeper into her mouth, and, at the edges of her vision, she could make out his hand clutching at the bedsheets.

"Stop!" he said after a moment. "I can't keep my bear under control." He eased her off him, and, in a deft movement, he got to his knees, and turned her around. Unexpectedly, she was now on her hands and knees. She'd always hated doing it doggy-style, embarrassed by the size of her behind, but Logan stroked the globes of her ass, whispering words of appreciation.

"You look so sexy like this, Dina," he murmured. "You have such a lovely round ass. I love your curves so much." The touch of his hands was soothing, and then gently arousing. She found herself arching her back, to encourage him to caress her more firmly. His fingers moved in circles, edging closer and closer to her sensitive labia. He was close, yet tantalizingly just out of reach. She gave a sigh of frustration, realizing at the same moment that he was deliberately teasing her.

"Be patient," he whispered, with a chuckle. She didn't feel patient. Her clit was already throbbing, and that telltale ache had begun deep inside her – a sign that she would soon be wet and ready for him. When both of his thumbs ran the length of her labia, her body jolted. He caressed her outer labia for several, maddening minutes, making her wetter and more hungry for him, before he moistened a finger in her juices, reached around in front of her thigh and touched her clit. She jumped again, harder than before. Her clit was like a live wired. At the same time, she felt his cock lightly pushing at her entrance. She groaned and arched her back further, and, in one movement, he was in. She gasped at being so suddenly filled by him. It was almost more than she could cope with.

Keeping his finger on her clit, softly circling, he began to move in and out of her. As he made slow, measured thrusts, Dina lowered her head onto her hands, and pressed her hand over her mouth. What Logan was doing to her felt so intense that she had to restrain herself from screaming. Her pussy walls were on fire, his cock turning them to liquid heat. Her muscles gripped his cock, each thrust sending them into tiny spasms. His thrusts quickened, and became harder, each one filling her to the hilt, his pelvis butting deliciously against her ass. Before long, the spasms turned into a violent tremor, and she held her breath, feeling like she was falling through space. One hard thrust knocked her over the edge, and she exploded in an intense, powerful orgasm, beginning at her clit, and detonating in waves deep inside her.

Logan took her orgasm as a sign to fuck her even harder, and she collapsed on her front, helpless, as he pumped in and out of her unrelentingly. As with the previous night, she came again and again, and, as she hit one, extra strong climax, Logan came too, rasping and growling in her ear.

Afterwards, he stayed on top of her, kissing her back and the nape of her neck.

"That was even hotter than last night, Dina, which I didn't

think was possible," he murmured. "I didn't know mating could be so intense. You're mine, all mine. I can't wait for the day that I fill you with my seed, and you bear our first cubs. I can't wait to make love to you while you're pregnant, your belly gently swelling with our babies." Dina wriggled with delight. She couldn't wait either. She was so ready to have Logan as her lifelong mate, and bear his cubs.

Logan was as good as his word. Dina didn't leave his place all of the following week. They stayed holed up in his cozy cabin, having rough, tender, energetic sex. He attended to her every need, cooking her amazing meals from his overstocked fridge, all of which had a strong meat focus. She ate deer, wild boar, moose and rabbit, all cooked to perfection.

On the following Saturday, Dina woke up to the sound of a beeper going.

"What's that?" she said drowsily, rubbing her eyes. When she opened them fully, she saw that Logan was already out of bed, pulling his clothes on.

"It's an alert. It means that there's a fire emergency somewhere in the forest, and my boys and I have to go deal with it."

"Is it bad?" she said, pulling herself into a sitting position.

"No. We just have to watch out for forest fires. It probably means that someone lit a campfire somewhere they shouldn't have." He walked over and kissed her on her forehead. "It's still early. Go back to sleep, sweetheart, and I'll wake you in a couple of hours with breakfast."

"Ok," she said uncertainly. As he crashed out of the cabin,

she lay back down, not thinking she'd fall back to sleep at all. But, within minutes, she was sound asleep again.

When Dina next awoke, it was to the sound of animal growls and snorts. She sat up quickly. *What is that?* She drew the curtain aside, but couldn't see anything unusual, so she pulled on the shirt Logan had been wearing the night before and rushed into the living room to look out of the window. What she saw made her jaw drop.

There were maybe eight huge bears fighting each other right in front of the window. Her heart began to beat fast, and she stifled a small scream. They were wrestling each other, tumbling around in the dirt, and their mouths were open, revealing sharp, white teeth. What the hell was she supposed to do? She wished Logan was here to help her. *Hold on, they're not actually fighting that aggressively.* As she forced herself to calm down, she saw that they were actually tumbling around like puppies. *They're playing! I didn't know adult bears did that. But then, what do I know about bears?* She pulled the curtain a little wider, and one of the bears paused mid-wrestle and looked right at her. It was a black bear, with these really intense, soulful eyes. As she watched, it came right up to the window, and pressed a paw against the glass. The paw was huge, with a large black pad, five smaller pads, and five sharp black claws. *It's Logan, of course it is*, her rational mind told her, although her heart was still pumping double time. Tense with nerves, she stepped away from the window, and walked to the front door. She opened it cautiously, and the bear was there, on the veranda, standing a little back from the door.

"Logan?" she whispered. The bear walked forward on all four paws, stretched its long muzzle towards her hand, and gave it a lick. She lifted her hand, still trembling a little, and placed it on the bear's head. Its fur – Logan's fur – was so soft and luxuriant. Growing more confident, she stroked his ears, and his muzzle, and his cute leathery nose. He turned his head in the direction of the other bears, and she followed his gaze. He gave a little bark, and they stopped rolling around in the dirt, got to their feet, backed up onto their hind legs and raised a paw. They were waving to her. They were all the guys she'd met at the garden party. Not that she could identify them individually, but it was them: Logan's clan. She waved back at them, and they returned to their tumbles. Logan stepped closer to the door, and nosed it wide open. Slipping past her, he walked into the cabin. Dina followed him hesitantly, and closed the door.

As she stood and watched, something began to change in his bear's body. His fur seemed to be disappearing. His head was shrinking, the muzzle shortening. His torso became tighter, more compact, while his limbs lengthened. Then it happened in the blink of an eye: he had human skin, and his muscles rippled; there was the sound of bones cracking, followed by a loud crunch and a kind of whoosh. And he was standing on two feet: a naked man. Dina ran over to Logan and wrapped her arms around him. Her eyes stung with emotion. Logan squeezed her tight, gently rubbing her back.

"I'm so sorry for scaring you, baby," he said tenderly.

"I wasn't scared," she whispered. He laughed. "Dina, I could smell it on you. You can't hide things like that from me, you know!" She looked up at him.

"I'm sorry. I was so happy to finally see you as a bear; I didn't want you to think I didn't like it. I was a little scared at first, but as soon as I understood it was you, it was fine."

"Good," he said, stroking her face. "I felt like this was the only thing missing from our pair bonding. Now we're complete." He lifted her chin with his thumb, so she was looking him in the eye. "Dina, I love you," he said.

"Oh, Logan, I love you too," she replied, eyes bright with tears of happiness.

"You do?" he whispered, as if he could scarcely believe it.

"I do. My feelings have been growing for you every day, as we've been spending all this time together and getting to know each other so well. And now I feel like we're so closely joined, we could never be parted."

"It's true, baby. We never will be," he replied, dipping his head, and drawing her into a long, tender kiss.

After what felt like hours, Logan drew back.

"God, you must think I'm a disgusting bear," he said. "I've been running around all morning, and here I am, touching you and I haven't even had a shower!" Dina laughed in delight.

"You smell great to me," she said. He smelled earthy and spicy – his usual exciting masculine scent. "But what happened with the fire?"

"Ah, just some idiot starting a fire by dropping a cigarette butt into a litter bin. We put it out easily. But if it hadn't been reported to us quickly, it would've been a different story," he said, shaking his head. "Now, I'm going for a shower. Want to join me?"

"I'd love to!" Dina said, eyes lighting up.

CHAPTER 6

Three months later

The town hall looked beautiful. The clan had worked so hard at turning it into the perfect space for both humans and shifters to celebrate, and they'd done an amazing job. There was a huge barbecue, and plenty of outside seating for everyone to hang out and relax. There was a jazz band, of course, and a full bar. The sun was shining, the sky was a perfect blue, and a few of the trees were turning to russet gold, signifying that fall wasn't far off.

Dina looked around in wonder. As a little girl, she'd thought she'd get married in the town hall, but when she'd grown up, the chances of that happening seemed slimmer and slimmer. And now here she was, being united with the most amazing guy in the world.

She'd made out to her friends that she and Logan had

married spontaneously during a weekend away in Vegas. They couldn't have a legal marriage, because he was a shifter and didn't have a regular birth certificate. They'd already had a shifter-only ceremony in the forest with the clan. It had been ancient and mysterious, involving complicated rites. Now, they were having a symbolic ceremony with all their friends and family. Dina's mom had been crying the entire time, and her dad looked like he was going to burst out of pride. Once they'd seen the venue looking so beautiful, Melissa and Kristin had forgiven her for apparently not including them in her wedding. She knew they'd understand once the shifter secret was revealed to them. They were her bridesmaids of course, along with Lauren. They were all wearing mint-green dresses in raw silk, cut in different styles to flatter their figures. Lauren's dress had been the most challenging to design, as she was almost six months pregnant, and her baby bump was getting big. She was blooming, her skin glowing with health, and she looked deliriously happy.

Dina stood in a spot where no-one could see her, looking at all the happy guests waiting for the ceremony to begin. Logan came up behind her and wrapped his arms around her.

"Are you ready, baby?" he asked, gently rubbing her belly. She wasn't yet beginning to show, but she could feel the new life inside her, alive and kicking, and growing day by day.

"I'm more than ready, Logan," she said. She lifted her chin, and he leaned over her shoulder and kissed her tenderly. He looked so handsome in his gray suit and button-down white shirt. Dina was wearing a stunning white satin dress, and a headdress with a long train.

As they walked out into the garden together, all eyes turned on them. Dina looked from one friend and family member to another, and her heart almost burst with happiness. They reached the end of a flower-strewn aisle that the clan had created for them, and the girls took their place behind her, lifting up her train.

Tamika was waiting at the other end of the aisle. Dina and Logan were making out to all the human guests that she was an official wedding celebrant, and she looked the part, in a striking white suit. The jazz band began to play the wedding march, and they walked down the aisle slowly, Dina wanting to savor every single second of it. They stopped in front of Tamika, beneath an arch entwined with passionflowers, just like the one at the garden party.

Shyly, they spoke their vows to each other, a simpler version of the ones they'd spoken at the shifter ceremony, where they'd promised to be each other's life-long mate. When they'd each said *"I do"* – the two little words that completed their union – Logan lifted Dina's veil and kissed her. Their friends and family broke out into clapping and cheering.

"Congratulations, darling!" Tamika's husky English voice boomed, and Dina hugged her. She knew she'd be grateful to her forever for connecting her with Logan. Then she turned to her bridesmaids and hugged them too. She looked from Melissa to Kristin with excitement. Once the shifter ceremony was complete, she was allowed to share the secret with either one of them. She'd been too busy preparing for the human ceremony to have time to do this yet, but once she and

Logan returned from their honeymoon in Mexico, it would be top of her list. The only problem was figuring out which one to tell.

THE END

READ THE NEXT BOOKS IN THE SERIES

Shiftr: Swipe Left For Love (Books 2-5)

The next instalment in the series features books 2-5. Find out how the little paw-print Shiftr dating app helps Kristin, Melissa, Andrea and Lori discover their happy-ever-afters.

Get at arianahawkes.com/shiftr

MATEMATCH OUTCASTS SERIES

MateMatch Outcasts: a matchmaking agency for beasts, and the women tough enough to love them.

If you're looking for more matchmaking stories, you may want to check out my *MateMatch Outcasts* series.

★★★★★ *"Absolutely Freaking Fantastic!"*

★★★★★ *"A super **exciting, funny, thrilling, suspenseful and steamy** shifter romance series. The characters jump right off the page!"*

★★★★★ *"Tons of heart, drama and passion!"*

Get at arianahawkes.com/matematch-outcasts

THANK YOU!

Hi, welcome to the world of Shiftr and thank you so much for reading Dina and Logan's story! I really hope you enjoyed it and if so please consider leaving a review; even if it's only a line or two, it'll make all the difference, and it will be greatly appreciated <3.

There are fourteen more *Shiftr: Swipe Left For Love* books waiting for you! The next instalment in the series features books 2-5. You can get it at arianahawkes.com/shiftr.

If you enjoy mail-order bride books, check out my *MateMatch Outcasts* series. It's set in Ragtown, a small former ghost town, deep in the mountains. It's a secretive place, closed-off to the outside world, and that's exactly how its broken, screwed-up inhabitants like it - until someone establishes MateMatch, a secret dating agency, and starts delivering mail order brides to the town. You can get the books at arianahawkes.com/matematch-outcasts.

If you like to be notified of new releases, sign up for my mailing list at arianahawkes.com/mailinglist. You can also follow me on BookBub at bookbub.com/authors/ariana-hawkes

Thanks again for reading – and for all your support!

Yours,
 Ariana Hawkes

ALSO BY ARIANA HAWKES

Shifter Dating App Romances
Shiftr: Swipe Left for Love – Book 1
Shiftr: Swipe Left for Love – Books 2-5
Shiftr: Swipe Left for Love – Books 6-8
Shiftr: Swipe Left for Love – Books 9-12
Shiftr: Swipe Left for Love – Books 13-15

MateMatch Outcasts
Grizzly Mate (MateMatch Outcasts Book 1)
Protector Mate (MateMatch Outcasts Book 2)
Rebel Mate (MateMatch Outcasts Book 3)
Monster Mate (MateMatch Outcasts Book 4)
Dragon Mate (MateMatch Outcasts Book 5)
Wild Mate (MateMatch Outcasts Book 6)

Fire Trails (Reverse harem romance)
In collaboration with K.N. Knight
Of Ashes And Sin (Fire Trails Book 1)
Queen Of Ashes (Fire Trails Book 2)

Shifterhood
Tiger's Territory (Shifterhood Book 1)

In Dragn Protection

Ethereal King (In Dragn Protection Book 1)

Boreas Reborn (In Dragn Protection Book 2)

Wounded Wings (In Dragn Protection Book 3)

Broken Hill Bears

Bear In The Rough (Broken Hill Bears Book 1)

Bare Knuckle Bear (Broken Hill Bears Book 2)

Bear Cuffs (Broken Hill Bears Book 3)

Christmas Bear Shifter Romances

Winter Bearland

Hill Bear Christmas

Three Shifter Christmas

Ultimate Bear Christmas Magic Box Set

Bear All I Want For Christmas Boxed Set

Bear Home For Christmas

Bear Christmas Magic

Bear My Perfect Gift

Polar Bears' Christmas

Standalone books

Lost To The Bear

Ravished by the Ice Palace Pack

Your free book is waiting!

A 4.5-star rated, comedy romance featuring one kickass roller derby chick, two scorching-hot Alphas, and the naughty nip that changed their lives forever.

The only thing missing from Aspen Richardson's life is a man who will love her just the way she is. In the small town she calls home, bullies from the past remain, making her wonder if it's ever going to happen. But, things are about to change in a major way, as the secret Aspen's parents have been keeping from her comes out…

"This book definitely needs to be added to your MUST read list – you will quickly fall in love with this steamy and fast paced story."

Get your free book at arianahawkes.com/freebook

ABOUT THE AUTHOR

USA Today bestselling author Ariana Hawkes writes spicy romantic stories with lovable characters, plenty of suspense, and a whole lot of laughs. She told her first story at the age of four, and has been writing ever since, for both work and pleasure. She lives in Massachusetts with her husband and two huskies.

Sign up for updates at arianahawkes.com/mailinglist.

www.facebook.com/arianahawkes
www.twitter.com/arianahawkes
ariana@arianahawkes.com

Made in United States
Troutdale, OR
12/08/2025